As Regards Mrs Graham

Ellen Campbell Barker

D1522833

2019

Table of Contents

Graham Family

Capt. George Graham b. 1835

m. Lettie Compton b. 1851

Pearl	Amanda	Carrie	Olivine	Flora	Virginia (Ginna)	Stuart	Charles
b.1873	b. 1875	b. 1876	b. 1878	b.1881	b. 1883	b. 1891	b. 1894
		m. Jefferson Carter			m. Hayden Graham		
					b. 1885		

Hayden Jr	Frances	Bascom	Henry
b.1913	b.1916	b.1919	b.1925

Cummings Family

John Cummings, b. 1858

m. Ada Teegarden b. 1862

Andrew	Farley
b. 1885	b. 1887
m Mae Foster	
b. 1886	

Julian	Annette	Adelaide
b.1912	b.1918	b.1919

Allison Family

Ez Allison b.1867

m. Parthenia Mullins b. 1869

Ella Rose b.1911

Part I

"…fundamentally, I'm interested in memory because it's a filter through which we see our lives, and because it's foggy and obscure, the opportunities for self-deception are there.
In the end, as a writer, I'm more interested in what people tell themselves happened rather than what actually happened."

— *Kazuo Ishiguro*

The Grahams of Carver County VA

February 14, 1911

Under a heap of quilts and blankets, a woman stirs in her sleep and almost awakens. Turning slightly, she sinks back into a dream of early summer and damp earth.

After some minutes or hours, the scrape of a chair in the kitchen below, the smell of ham frying, and the demands of her sore body combine to drown all dreams. She sits up in bed with slow care. She swings her feet to the floor. She is wearing a pair of her father's woolen stockings, and, to avoid slipping on the old oak boards, she steadies herself by holding onto the bed's foot post. She uses the commode brought up from her father's sickroom.

Dampening her hands in the wash bowl just enough to wipe the sleep out of her eyes, she dries her face and hands with the small towel edged with tatting. She picks up her hairbrush from the bureau and sits on the side of the bed and begins to loosen her hair from its braid.

The bedroom door opens with its familiar creak. "Ginna, the snow has piled up two feet or more. I don't expect your husband will come calling today." Ollie gently restores the plait and says, "Slip back under the covers now, and I'll tuck this water bottle in with you. Do you want it at your feet or your back? I'll bring up some coffee and biscuits after while." She closes the door quietly behind her as if the younger woman were not already awake.

Submitting without protest but still sitting up in bed, Ginna stares straight ahead at the mirror over the bureau. She whispers: "Murderer."

Olivine and Virginia Graham were the fourth and sixth daughters of George and Lettie Compton Graham of Maple Grove, a rural community in the southwestern corner of Virginia, near the small town of Clayton Hill. In this valley, as

2

in all parts of the world, there was a social hierarchy. The extended Graham family sat firmly at the top of Carver County's hierarchy. It was said of the Grahams that they thought they were better than everyone else so they had to marry each other or stay single. A family wit of a later generation was reported to have said, "Thank God they finally built a road over the mountain or we would all be imbeciles."

Among the three older daughters, only one, Carrie, had married, and to a man considered unworthy of the family. Ollie said, "Everyone says what a hard worker Jeff Carter is. Jeff this and Jeff that. Well, he sure kept Carrie busy having a baby every other year. I don't think Papa or Mother ever really accepted their daughter marrying someone from a family like the Carters, never mind how hard he worked or how many acres he managed to buy." As a matter of fact, Ollie had a lot to say on the subject of appropriate behavior, especially in regard to suitable marital alliances.

"You young folks joke about us Grahams marrying each other, but you don't understand how things were back in those days. There were so few quality families within courting range that our cousins were the most natural sweethearts to be had. For Pearl and Amanda and me, well, there was just no man we would have, Graham or not. Look at Thomas Jefferson and some of them back in Eastern Virginia. They all married within the family. It was what well-bred people did! So don't go acting like it's something to be ashamed of," she later told her niece, Frances.

The two eldest daughters were school teachers living in Clayton Hill with their aunt. The sister between Ollie and Virginia was afflicted with mental retardation and seizures. She was referred to as *Poor Dear Flora.*

Two younger brothers, Stuart and Charles, came along when their mother was in her forties.

George Graham was widely referred to as "Captain Graham." According to Ollie, "Our papa was a wholly respectable man. He carried himself perfectly straight all his days in spite of unrelenting pain in his legs. He left college at Hampden-Sydney against the wishes of his father to join the Carver County Greys. He was badly injured in a fall from his horse at Dry Creek in

4

'63, and returned to his post, probably much too soon. I well remember Mother having to cut his boots off because his feet and ankles swelled so. He led men from this area through the war. I suppose I should say, "*War Between the States*." There have been two or three others since, haven't there?"

'Papa petted Virginia something awful because she was the baby for years, until the boys came along. You will recall that your Aunt Pearl and Aunt Amanda were the oldest, and they became teachers. Long before they finished their own schooling, they played teacher to us younger ones. We got a head start on our primary lessons. That would be Carrie, me and Ginna. Poor dear Flora was not ever able to play with us. Mother had her hands full caring for Flora and then, lo and behold, Stuart and Charles appeared. It was simply impossible for Mother to put the damper on Ginna's willfulness or persuade Papa to do so."

Living at the home place in Maple Grove were Captain Graham and Lettie, Ollie, Flora, Ginna, Stuart and Charles. Many years later, Charles was to describe their lives,

"Ollie and some of the others like to think we were a little bit better than other folks in the valley. I reckon that was a common idea among the Grahams several generations back. When you are growing up, you don't have the least idea of how anybody outside your family or your neighbors is thinking. I don't believe it any more but, for a long time, I probably did think we were something special.

Remember that Ginna was about ten years older than me and so a couple of years closer in age to Stuart. Pearl and them were like aunts to us even if they were sisters. Practically by the time I was old enough to know what was going on around me, I guess Carrie was married or at least courting. Ollie would sometimes teach us some children's games, when she could stop preaching to us for a minute. But Ginna, now she could be a fun or a holy terror.

Papa was old-fashioned strict. He would beat the fire out of me and Stuart, usually on account of something

Ginna had gotten us into. Well, that's not quite true. He found plenty of other reasons to take the strap to us.

Never forget the day when I was about five or six and Ginna called us up to her room. Said she had something to show us. Stuart wasn't much smarter than me so we both jumped at the chance to visit "her majesty's chamber." She told us to be real quiet and not let anybody know were up there. Ollie shared a room with her, but Ollie was most always helping Mama in the kitchen. So we tiptoe up there and close the door, kind of holding our breath for excitement. Before we hardly got the door closed, Ginna starts pulling her dress over her head and then pulls her shift right down to her waist.

"Well?" she asks.

"Well, what?" Stuart says.

"I am getting bosoms!" Ginna whispers.

"Don't look like it to me," Stu replies.

Just that minute, Ollie comes through the door and throws a hissy that could be heard all over the house, maybe to the next county. Of course, before the end of the day, we boys had our tails beat for the terrible sin of having seen our sister strip half-naked. I don't believe Ginna was punished at all. Probably had to start wearing grown-up underclothes after that.

We did have some good adventures on account of Ginna though. She was the one who showed us the cave on our farm where the rebel soldiers mined and hid salt peter to make gunpowder during the Civil War. I found an old bent-up belt buckle in there that I have to this day. I suspect that Papa must have known about the cave, but we liked to think it was our big secret. We knew for sure that if we were found out going in there, we'd be in big trouble. We boys, that is.

Ginna would make Christmas time great fun. Some other holidays too. She would help us, when we were real small, make presents for our folks. Working on these little doodads got us even more excited about what ole Santie might bring us, I guess, because we thought we were showing the Christmas Spirit and earning some more loot for our socks. While Mama and Ollie would be cooking, and poor old Flora sitting in the corner with her scraps of rags, Ginna would put up the most outlandish decorations. Everyone in the valley thought our house was the best place to be around Christmas.

Back in those days, we didn't celebrate the 4th of July much, like folks do now. Decoration Day was when we showed our respect for those who had gone before, especially soldiers. On Decoration Day, Papa would put on his old uniform and, with the other veterans, hold a service of remembrance at the church, followed by dinner on the ground. Families would decorate the graves in the church graveyard and in family cemeteries, which is where they had done most of the burying back years ago. It was always good to be with relatives and friends you might not have seen for a year, and Ginna loved more than anything to organize decorations and special music. You might think Decoration Day would be a sad occasion but it gave me a feeling that I was connected to the souls that had preceded me and souls to follow. It wasn't like now where they haul a body off to the funeral parlor. In those days, the dead were laid out in their own home and friends would come by to visit. Some even sat up all night. People today don't want to think about death but I saw so much of it during the Great War, and since, that I know you have to make your peace with it sooner or later because it is going to win.

I think Ginna had right smart of admirers. A brother can't judge, especially a younger one, but I wouldn't say she was a beauty. She just had a way about her that made people want to be around her and do what pleased her."

Ollie and Ginna, like the three oldest sisters, attended Anderson Female Institute, in nearby Abingdon. A sort of finishing school for young ladies, it also offered teacher preparation.

"When I graduated, I was needed at home to help Mother, and was perfectly happy to do so. I did not have the desire to teach school like Pearl and Amanda, much less to become a farmer's wife with a houseful of children like Carrie. Looking after the boys and Flora, along with my duties at church, provided more than enough occupation for me," Ollie said.

Unlike Ollie, when Ginna finished at the Institute she didn't seem to know what to do with herself. She was terribly restless for some while after she came home. She began painting furiously for months, and then started writing plays. She seemed to sleep no more than a few hours a day. The following spring, Ginna fell ill. Although no specific diagnosis was ever named, the doctor did not consider it to be particularly severe. When several weeks passed and she did not seem to be recovering, their mother had the doctor back. He determined that the problem was her nerves, and only rest would bring her around.

It was Ollie's duty to wait on her sister, and she resented it. "Each afternoon after dinner I would go to our room and try to interest her in a book. I was careful to choose something cheerful, but, more often than not, she would turn her face away and say she just needed to sleep a while. This, after having slept most of the morning and picking at a tray of food brought to her by me! I tell you she tried my patience. When I attempted to talk to Mother about it, she would only remind me that Dr. Thorpe said we must give her time."

Autumn 1905
<u>Ginna Meets August Stern</u>

It was not at all unusual, back in the early years of the 20th century, for families to lose a child to illness, often several children to the same illness. The family of George Graham considered itself blessed to have lost only two infants at birth. Scarlet fever, or scarlatina, was a perplexing disease, the course of which varied from barely noticeable to fatal. Because of his tendency to pleurisy and croup, when Stuart began to show symptoms of Scarlet Fever soon after his 15th birthday, Dr. Thorpe undertook a campaign to be certain the health of this Graham son was protected. Though Stuart protested that he did "not feel all that rough" in spite of his ulcerated throat, the doctor ordered that his head be shaved because, inevitably, his hair would fall out. That having been done, Stuart ceased to complain about the accompanying decree that he stay out of school for the rest of the term. He would gladly die before showing himself to his schoolmates shorn of his wavy brown hair.

Ginna was lingering under the rest prescribed by the doctor for her nervous malady. Her brother's illness, surprisingly, motivated her to set aside her novels and poetry. She announced that she would oversee Stuart's lessons in hopes he would be able to progress on schedule with his classmates when the new term began in January.

Because she had been a precocious student, the particular favorite of most of her teachers, Ginna did not have any hesitancy about seeking out Stuart's teacher, August Stern. From her brothers' references to their teacher, the image she had of Mr. Stern was indeed stern, an old man with a way of speaking that reflected an outsider's background. She pictured him with a straggly mustache and tobacco stained teeth.

As soon as Stuart was feeling a bit stronger, Ginna made her way to the school one afternoon at about the time the pupils were leaving for the day. She encountered her youngest brother Charles in a clump of boys running to be the first off the school ground. He gave her a look that dared her to acknowledge him and hurried to walk home with the Clark boys and Hays Dean.

The essence of school-oiled floors, chalk, sweat, and mildewed books-greeted Ginna as she approached the front door. As she tried to maintain her balance with the primary age children now pushing past her on both sides, she felt herself being enveloped by something she hadn't realized she missed.   She walked down the familiar hallway to the back of the building where the classroom for the older students was.

August Stern was stacking up his books and papers when she tapped lightly on the open door of his classroom, one of four in the building. He glanced up, expecting to see one of his more timid pupils needing help with an arithmetic problem. Ginna was shocked. Indeed, he did look stern, but he was by no means old, maybe 10 years older than she, the mustache was neatly trimmed. About his teeth she had no idea because he had not yet opened his mouth to greet her with a smile or words. He was a smallish man, not much taller than Ginna, with what could be called a trim build. He was looking at Ginna as if surprised, and not pleasantly so.

Finally, Ginna said, "Excuse me, Mr. Stern, for bothering you. I am Virginia Graham, Stuart's sister. I was hoping to speak to you about how Stuart might be able to continue his school work at home to be able to finish out the fall term."

"There was no particular certainty that Stuart would pass the term even if he had not been prevented from attendance by his recent illness," Stern finally said, in his peculiar accent.

Ginna felt her face heat up like a gas lamp. How dare the man speak this way about a child who was near death only a week ago? Though Stuart might not be a scholar, he was a Graham and had the family cleverness to see him through the most difficult subjects when sufficiently motivated.

"Stuart has a good mind but not a good head on him. He would rather entertain his classmates with his pranks than apply himself to his lessons."

Stern cleared his throat. He realized that he had offended the rather handsome sister of his smart but lazy student. He would never understand southerners, especially the women.

When Ginna still did not reply, he went on, "Though I must admit he has been known to amuse me, try as I might to keep him from being aware of the fact. He is clever!"

"Perhaps we could let him work on some of his history lesson at home. That seems to be the area he inclines to be most interested in. Take it slow, you see, so as not to wear him out. See how he gets along."

He picked up the history text book and flipped through to the chapters covered in the recent weeks. Hurriedly jotting a few notes of instruction while Ginna watched, Stern continued, "Now, Miss Graham, perhaps when Stuart feels up to it, he might begin reading these chapters paying particular attention to the items I have noted here. Ummm. I certainly would not want him to undertake too much at once. His recovery is the main thing, of course."

Poor Stuart was less than grateful for his sister's sudden ambition to bolster his academic career. For one thing, he felt he barely knew her. She had never seemed to pay him much mind, being either wrapped up in some compelling project or "swooning" in her boudoir, as he liked to say. At least Ollie occasionally would play pranks on him or Charles when she wasn't beating them over the head with the Gospel. The older sisters seemed more of an age with their mother. Now he had Ginna acting like his private tutor, and he didn't like it one bit.

A few days after her initial consultation with Mr. Stern, Ginna returned with Stuart's grudgingly completed notes on the areas of emphasis Stern had indicated. "I am afraid my brother is still feeling very weak much of the time, but he did finish the reading assignment you sent home" she offered as she handed the tablet to the teacher. "I discussed the chapters with him at some length and do believe he is developing an interest in history after all."

"Perhaps delirium brought on by fever?" Stern responded, meeting her gaze and then suddenly and deliberately smiling to be sure she knew this was an attempt at humor.

Ginna was speechless for a few seconds longer than spontaneous conversation would justify while she decided whether to be furious with this ill-bred person.

"There is that possibility, I suppose," she finally answered with a shadow of a smile of her own.

Relieved, Stern looked over the notes and proceeded to make further assignments in history and geometry. "Do you think Stuart's father can help him with the geometry if he runs into difficulty? Or you, perhaps, have studied the subject?"

"Why, yes, in this very classroom. Under Mr. McDougall. But that was some time ago, and, I must say, mathematics was never my particular forte' as is true for most girls."

"True in many cases, perhaps the majority. My own sister, however, is a mathematics teacher in New Jersey."

"Is she indeed?" Ginna replied, picturing the worst sort of mannish Yankee suffragette.

That evening, Ginna reviewed Stuart's geometry text book to refresh her memory and, being as it was mid-way of the first term of the course, she was able to catch up at least to the varieties of triangles, the relations of radius, diameter and circumference. Having brushed up on the subject to that extent, she proceeded to bedevil Stuart for two or three days until it was time for her to return to school with his work.

Over the next few weeks, Ginna discovered a heretofore buried fascination with Latin grammar and the geography of Indochina in addition to plane geometry that left Stuart dreading her return from school with his assignments. She pressed the convalescent to complete his work so adamantly that he begged Dr. Thorpe to let him go back to school so he could get some rest.

Now, when Ginna arrived at the school after the final bell rang, she most often found August Stern standing, with his hair appearing damp from a recent combing, a slight smile on his face and a chair pulled up for Ginna to sit down next to his desk so that they could go over Stuart's recent efforts. It was becoming apparent to both of them, though unacknowledged, that the furthest thing from their minds was whether Stuart passed the term. Oh, he would pass of course, but that was hardly the point any more.

One Friday in November, when the weather had turned suddenly, Ginna wore her heavy cape and bundled her neck with her father's scarf for the half mile walk to the school. Stern hung the cape in the cloakroom as the woodstove had made the classroom uncomfortably warm. They could hear the departing children hooting and laughing as a few flakes of snow began to fall. The two adults got up to look out the window at the mountain behind the school already showing snow at its very top. Stern opened the window to admonish some little ones to go home directly. "Let your mama know you are home and then go back out to play. David Price, did you hear me? Go on home now."

They settled down to go over Stuart's lessons but the increasing volume of snowfall distracted both of them. Stern had a buggy ride of three miles to his boarding house, in the opposite direction of the Graham home.

"Shouldn't we be on our way, Miss Graham. I can take you home in the buggy?"

"Oh goodness no. I love a walk in the snow, and it's barely even sticking yet. I will run on so you can close up."

"Let me get your wrap then." Stern went into the cloakroom to fetch the cape and scarf. As he lifted them off the hook, he was surprised to hear footsteps behind him. Ginna stood very still while he placed the cape on her shoulders. When she didn't make a move to take the scarf, he placed that on her head and began to wrap the ends around her neck in the way she had it arranged upon her arrival. He gave a little laugh as he fiddled with the scarf.

"You will certainly need to be able to see to make your way," he said pushing the scarf back a bit from the sides of her face.

And then, of course, they kissed, the longest, most welcome kiss that was ever to occur in either of their lives. Ginna, in spite of the impropriety of the moment, felt not so much passion as a sense of being welcomed to a place she had always longed to be. Completely safe. Completely happy. Nothing outside of that cloakroom would ever matter. She could die right that moment with no regret.

Stern's feelings were primal in a different way. After a few more kisses, he chivalrously pulled away. Taking her hands in his, he managed to say, "Now you really should go. May I, shall I, speak to your father about permission to call on you?"

"Oh, I do think that would be the thing to do!" Ginna answered, with a radiant smile.

By the time Christmas vacation was approaching, and with it the beginning of the new term and Stuart's return to school, a few stolen kisses in the cloakroom had become a common occurrence. Ginna, having grown up on the farm, was aware of the biology of reproduction. Her upbringing, typical of girls of her class, had steered completely clear of discussion of the feelings attendant to that biology. There was romance and there was common behavior, and never the two should meet. Now Ginna knew the secret, the source of poetry and song since the beginning of time.

For the first few days of Christmas vacation, Ginna dreamed deliriously of a life with August. The morning of Christmas Eve, she observed from her bedroom window that he drove up the road in his little cart and knocked on the front door. She could hardly make out the voices over the sound of her pounding heart but she knew that he and Papa were speaking in the parlor. Her father did not mention the visit, and she thought it best not to ask. The week that followed was nearly unbearable.

When school resumed, she believed it was only a matter of time before August would officially begin his courtship. After the first day of the new school year, at the supper table with her mother and father, Stuart and Charles, as well as Ollie, Ginna fought to keep her hands from shaking as she asked Stuart how he had fared the first day back at school after his long absence.

"Ah…I made it all right. Seems like I have kept up pretty well with all the lessons" Stuart said, as he buttered a biscuit. "Took a good while to get the stove going. Liked to froze."

"How do you like that new teacher?" Charles asked.

"I think she might be a little bit easier to please than old Stern," Stuart answered.

Ginna stopped breathing. Ollie glanced at her quickly and then down at her plate. Ginna's eyes immediately locked on her father.

"Yes, he seems to have gone to greener pastures back where he's from," was all that Captain Graham had to say. And it was enough. Ginna knew that, as a member of the school board, her father had seen to it that August Stern would not be around for more stolen kisses or anything else. Rising from the table, at which every member of the family seemed to find the simultaneous need to reach for their napkins and wipe the corners of their mouths, Ginna walked upstairs, removed her shoes and got into bed. There she stayed, more or less, for six months.

George Graham was a stubborn man and prideful man, but he loved his youngest daughter. He believed he had done the best thing for her when he dispatched August Stern. When he felt Ginna's rejection in the following months, he began to question his wisdom. Unlike her sisters, Pearl, Amanda, and Olivine, Ginna had a passionate nature. Captain Graham feared that it would lead to an unfortunate romance undertaken, in part, to repay his protectiveness. He also regarded his youngest daughter as the brightest of his children and, in fact, had always enjoyed her company more than any of the others.

By the following summer, a situation had arisen that prompted the old man to try to make amends. One evening, on a rare occasion when Ginna had joined the family for supper, he endured her usual cold two-word answers to his questions throughout the meal. As she got up to return to her room, he said, "Virginia, let me have a word with you on the porch." Lettie and the children always knew what such a request meant. It meant something serious was to be discussed, and no one else would be welcome. After a moment of hesitation during which Ginna glared at her father, she relented and made her way outside.

"Sit down," he said. "Virginia, I know your heart is hardened toward me. I felt that I had to save you from yourself. A father's duty is to protect his children, especially his daughters, from folly, not to mention the maintenance of our family's reputation. Perhaps someday you will see to forgive me. I hope and pray you will. But, meanwhile, I need, this family needs, you to direct your energy and good will toward those under this roof. Your mother has not told anyone, nor have I, but she will have to have a serious operation very soon. Dr. Thorpe needs to remove a dangerous tumor…a cancer."

Before Ginna could respond, he went on "Mother will not be able to take care of Flora as she has all these years. She won't be able to help lift her or bathe her. Ollie cannot undertake to assume all that responsibility as well as the cooking and looking after the boys. I hope you can see how very much we will need you to step in."

"Will Mother die?"

"Dr. Thorpe thinks it looks very bad, but Mother's faith is strong and she is convinced she will recover."

"Dear Papa, I will gladly do whatever is needed."

So began the rapprochement between George and Virginia Graham.

Within months, Lettie died, followed shortly by Flora, whose cries of "mamamama" haunted the memories of Captain Graham and his surviving children the rest of their lives.

1908-1909
The Clayton Hill Lending Library

When Ginna emerged from a brief period of mourning for her mother and sister, she took up the notion of establishing a lending library for the town of Clayton Hill. She didn't so much take up the notion as the notion took her over. She studied the Dewey Decimal System, and, having begun speaking to her father again, she spoke of little else.

Determined to find a room to house the library, Ginna first approached the ministers of the Methodist, Baptist, and Presbyterian churches in Clayton Hill. She was disappointed, but not defeated, when each, in turn, informed her that there would be no room available for secular works, that their own church libraries were sufficient for the needs of their flocks.

Since Ginna wanted eventually to be able to collect books of all sorts, including those which might promise some controversy, she soon realized her naivete' in having even briefly considered housing the library in a church.

Meanwhile, she went door to door, in town and on the outskirts, soliciting donations of any volumes the citizens might be willing to part with. She had accumulated more than two dozen, mostly old, worm-chewed, geographies and devotional publications by autumn and had promises of many more "when we get around to going through the shelves." She began to try to sell subscriptions from interested parties- and there were a few-to generate funds to buy new books.

Ginna began talking to businessmen, numbering five or six, in Clayton Hill. She counted on her cousin, Wallace Graham, to spare her a small room at the Barrel Works. Wallace pointed out that the books would be damaged by sawdust and damp. In truth, Wallace was wary of any scheme his cousin's daughter proposed. He had known her all her life and seen her enthusiasms wax and wane, sometimes affecting her younger brothers and his own children. Dr. Thorpe had advised Ginna to find some outlet for her energies, but even he could not find a closet or nook to hold a few books in his office on the corner.

"It would so behoove the citizens of this community to establish a library, no matter how modest," was the stated opinion of Mable Spratt, wife of the Presbyterian minister. Ginna organized a committee, consisting of Rev. and Mrs. Spratt, the school teacher Livia Tuttle, Ginna's reluctant sister Ollie, and two cousins, Louisa and Hayden Graham, to conduct a drive to bring the idea of a library to fruition. Louisa and Hayden, a bit younger than Ginna, and the children of Wallace Graham, had been bedazzled by her since childhood. Meetings were slightly contentious, with Ginna enthusiastic about such works as those of Henry and William James and others, particularly Louisa, preferring more edifying volumes. Ginna maintained a reasonably calm, if determined, demeanor as she worked with the committee on ideas for the library, still lacking a space or enough money to purchase more than a few volumes. Her father and other older adults began to come around, purchasing subscriptions and talking encouragingly about the project.

One evening, before the beginning of a scheduled meeting at the Presbyterian church, Ginna was arranging her notes when Hayden appeared on his own. He had always been the most backward of boys and blushed hectically when he managed to venture a comment during meetings. "Cousin Ginna. I have some news that I think will please you," he blurted rather loudly.

Footsteps of other members could be heard approaching so he hurried on, "Papa has found a little room at the Barrel Works! It was an old office up on the back that doesn't serve any purpose any more, and it doesn't even connect to the rest of the plant. It's small and the steps are rickety but, what do you think?" Rev. Spratt, Ollie, and Miss Tuttle entered the room to see the giddy Hayden and Ginna, who had just thrown her arms around his neck.

"We have a place! We have a place!" Ginna shouted. "At the Barrel Works. When can we go look at it, Hayden?"

The Clayton Hill Library, which has since evolved into a branch of the Carver County VA Public Library, was open two days a week, beginning in 1908. It was staffed by volunteers, including Ginna Graham, Louisa Graham, Livia Tuttle, and Mabel Spratt for the first few years. Though Ginna was sometimes considered overbearing by her colleagues, the work proceeded and the community was proud of having its own library. Its patronage was made up largely of its committee members and their families, but the occasional newcomer found his way to its shelves.

Ginna's family believed firmly that she had found her mission in life, at least until she married, if she were to eventually marry. She seemed to have outgrown her nervous afflictions.

Spring 1910
Jubilee Celebration
Clayton Hill Presbyterian Church

1910 was to be the 75th Anniversary of the founding of the Clayton Hill Presbyterian Church. Rev. Spratt was leaving for a new pastorate in Bluefield. Congregants began plans for the jubilee, to be held in the spring, as they anticipated the arrival of E.J. Sanders, a young graduate of Union Seminary. Sanders arrived in late February. Captain Graham and Ollie and Ginna were all heavily involved in preparations for the celebration, and Rev. Sanders was grateful that they relieved him of that responsibility so he could concentrate on the many expectations he placed upon himself serving his first church.

Ginna soon began finding it necessary to make frequent trips to the church, saying she could not do what was needed from home. She became so occupied with this work that she began to miss her volunteer days at the library. Her cousin Louisa was most displeased as they had already lost Mrs. Spratt when she left with her husband. Hayden filled in on some Saturdays but that did not ease Louisa's resentment. She was involved with the jubilee planning as well and felt that Ginna was attempting to impose her ideas without regarding the suggestions of others.

In addition to worship, Ginna proposed that the three-day event have attractions for all ages, saying that the little children would remember it for the rest of their lives. She had in mind games and contests, as well as music and food which had already been put on the agenda by the group. During a warm spell in late March she invited Rev. Sanders on a little jaunt around the near environs of the church to show him where a sack race, a scavenger hunt and a tug-of-war might be staged. While Sanders much preferred staying in his study to write sermons, he was helpless to resist "Miss Graham's" enthusiastic proposal. After the first foray, they made several other exploratory ventures. He learned that she was easy to talk to and shared his interests in philosophy and history.

While some were aware of Ginna's spending time with the minister, including her family, only the older ladies and young

Miss Louisa Graham were disapproving. Louisa fretted to her brother, "Ginna is not trying to take over the jubilee. She is trying to take over the minister. He hasn't even had time to meet many of the other congregants, much less go picnicking with them. She started that library, and now she has almost abandoned it like a mother turtle abandons her eggs."

"Now, Louisa, what do you know about the domestic habits of turtles? Ginna is just trying to make him feel welcome and to help him get to know Clayton Hill," Hayden said in an attempt to soothe his sister. He suspected that she wished to be in the running for the reverend's attentions, and the expressed concern about the library was exaggerated.

"If I know Ginna, she is helping him get to know Ginna Graham!"

Hayden tried to think of something to say in defense of Ginna, but found himself coming around to Louisa's point of view. He regarded Ginna with awe and had never presumed to contemplate wooing her, but, with the prospect of Rev. Sanders doing so, his instincts were beginning to emerge.

"I heard Dr. Thorpe is bringing in a young doctor to study under him for a year. Maybe he will take away some of the competition for Sanders," Hayden offered.

"Do you think I am in *competition* for the minister? The very idea! I have suitors, as you know, and do not need the minister or some doctor to come courting! You and I both need to keep the library running and keep Ginna from turning the jubilee into a play party. That is all I am saying, Hayden."

Hayden was called upon to assist Ginna with the planning for the children's activities. Their design of a scavenger hunt among the hiding places on the church grounds and in the cellar was the culmination of Hayden's heart's desire. The jubilee was a big success, and the children attending were to have fond memories of it as Ginna had predicted.

For Rev. Sanders, the memory of that spring and summer was to become the source of years of longing and regret for other reasons. He and his wife were to scrupulously avoid referring to his days at the Clayton Hill church in the interest of maintaining the fragile bond of their relationship.

Dr. Thorpe's young medical apprentice, Andrew Cummings, was introduced around during the celebratory weekend. The young ladies found him nice-looking but "dull as dishwater." Having met him at the library, Ginna considered Dr. Cummings anything but dull. She was entranced.

Following the jubilee, Ginna experienced a period of total exhaustion and took to her bed for over a week. Dr. Thorpe admonished her not to let herself get melancholy as she had in the past. He sent Dr. Cummings to follow-up several times.

Dr. Cummings reported that her spirits seemed to him to be excellent; she was just tired from all the work and suffering from a bad cold. Ginna Graham was unlike any woman Andrew had ever met. He was engaged to a young lady from Radford, but began to be troubled by frequent dreams of Miss Graham.

She was soon up and about, resuming her schedule at the library and frequenting the pastor's study at every opportunity. She called in at the doctor's office in late June with a vague complaint of numbness in her left hand, but upon finding Dr. Thorpe rather than Dr. Cummings available, she declared that feeling had returned and that it wouldn't be necessary to have an examination.

Captain Graham suffered an episode of palsy in September and was left somewhat debilitated. Ginna took it upon herself to be the main conduit of information about his treatment between the doctors and the family. Ollie devoted herself to his direct care.

The youngest of the Grahams, Charles, began college, but Stuart, at 20, was seemingly aimless, spending as much time as possible carousing with his friends in the nearby towns. Ollie noticed his behavior but was too concerned with their father's condition to pay much attention. The three oldest sisters, long out of the house, paid solicitous calls on their father but did not concern themselves with Ginna or Stuart.

1910
<u>Christmas Eve in Clayton Hill</u>

The young folks of the respectable valley families were gathered for a party at Burley and Gladys Thompson's house. Furniture had been pushed back to the walls, and the usual musicians were plying their fiddles and mandolins. A few couples made shy attempts at dancing but most laughed and talked and enjoyed simply being in a lively crowd on a holiday evening.

William Maples asked his wife Birdie to take a whirl but she sweetly declined, being as plump as a berry tart with her expected baby. Birdie said, "Why don't you try one of the old maids?" That would include the two Graham sisters, Ollie and Ginna, and Mary Foster. Since Ollie and Mary appeared to be deep in conversation and had not a speck of fun in them, William approached Ginna, who could often be counted upon to kick up some dust, unless she was in one of those nervous spells she had from time to time. William knew for a fact that Ginna's second cousin, Hayden Graham, thought she hung the moon and would have married her in an instant if she would have him.

Laughing brightly, Ginna accepted William's offer to dance, with a grateful raising of the chin to her friend Birdie. As it happened, William and Ginna danced two or three dances together that evening. Hayden showed up later but, as always, was too backward to dance with anyone.

That night in bed, like many married couples, William and Birdie compared notes about the party and its attendees. They had covered the subject, Birdie thought, when she attempted to settle herself into a more comfortable position for sleep.

"Bird," William whispered.

"Hmmm?" Birdie really was exhausted but William was a man of few words, and she would gladly stay awake all night for the opportunity of hearing some.

"Something about Ginna."

"What?"

"I shouldn't even say it."

"What?"

"Well, I have danced with her many a time and hugged her neck when we got married, you know?" He was quiet for a moment. "Sorry, Bird, I don't know. Maybe she is just getting ready to have another one of her nervous spells. She is different, that's all."

"I thought you were going to say she was wintering well. I never have known what to make of her. Poor thing."

February 6, 1911
Birth and Death

Ollie had slept in a little longer than usual. When she came into the kitchen, she was shocked to see it lamplit. Hearing a scratching sound near the cookstove, she was even more shocked to see Ginna's backside sticking out from behind it, vigorously moving back and forth. The stove had been moved a few inches and the chimney pipe looked dangerously close to coming loose.

"What in the nation are you doing Virginia?"

"I cleaned inside and outside the stove yesterday, and I got to thinking how nasty the floor must be under the feet so I moved it just a tiny bit to scrub under them." Ginna's voice was somewhat muffled by virtue of the fact that her head was behind the stove and also by the continuing scratch-scratch of the brush on the old floor. She straightened up to reach back to the bucket of soapy water behind her.

"Let me just rinse under this last bit and you can start breakfast."

"You are about to knock the stove pipe loose and then there'll be no breakfast today. Get yourself out of there." Ginna's industriousness frightened Ollie.

"Gonna make a stack cake and take over to the old folks at Gibsons' later on."

"Come on out Ginna," Ollie urged and was pleasantly surprised to see some progress in that direction.

"Oh lord, I think I am stuck," Ginna grunted.

Ollie said, "Surely not. Just stay straight."

"I am stuck, I tell you."

"Well, then let me get some lard and grease you up so you can slide out because I am not about to let you endanger that stove pipe any further."

Both sisters began to laugh and, in Ollie's case, laughed until she cried, using the dishtowel to wipe her face by the time Ginna had backed all the way out and taken Ollie's hand to stand up.

"Just be thankful Papa didn't come in here and see you like a heifer in a head catch."

Good as her word, Ginna made a molasses stack cake and started off that afternoon after dinner to walk across the fields to their neighbors. The treacherous false spring that often happens in February was upon them, and she put on her father's work boots to navigate the muddy low places she would encounter.

Ollie was pleased that Papa seemed to be feeling a bit stronger that day. He had eaten a good bit of dinner and even went out to the porch for a few minutes with a blanket over his knees to enjoy the afternoon sun. She fixed them a bite for supper, and he again seemed to have a good appetite.

Ginna refused supper and, in fact, complained when she returned from the Gibsons' of an upset stomach.

"You have worn yourself out," Ollie said when she went upstairs to look in on Ginna. "Oh, what is this? You have been sick." Ollie picked up the slop jar and quickly covered it.

Ginna was lying on the bed, turned away from Ollie. "Sick, sick," she said.

"Let me get you another pot and a washcloth. Anything else?"

Ginna's reply was a guttural groan.

Ollie had settled Papa into bed downstairs before she checked on Ginna again.

"Please Mommy help me" were the words she heard as she climbed the stairs to Ginna's room.

"I am hurting so bad Mommy."

"What hurts Ginna?"

"Legs. My legs. Back. God help me."

Ollie was accustomed to Ginna's sense of the dramatic but now she was truly alarmed.

"I'll send for Dr. Thorpe."

"No. God please help me."

Hurrying downstairs, Ollie summoned their brother Stuart from the back parlor.

"Get Dr. Thorpe. I don't know what's wrong with Ginna. I pray not a burst appendix. "

Seeing Stuart's down turned mouth, Ollie said, "Get up and go Stuart. I think there is something really wrong this time."

During the two hours she waited for the arrival of the doctor, Ollie was unable to help Ginna, or even remain in her presence for long. Ginna was beside herself, calling on her dead mother or using language Ollie had never heard, at least never heard from a female in their family. Ginna vomited again and Ollie tried to clean up, to wash Ginna's face but the force of Ginna's pain frankly frightened Ollie. She beat a path up and down the steps to be sure her father had not been awakened.

Finally, Stuart returned with Dr. Thorpe and Dr. Cummings in tow.

"She is awful sick to her stomach and hurting in her legs and back. I don't know what in the world…", Ollie said to the two physicians as they climbed the stairs.

Stuart quickly retreated. In fact, he went out the back door, Ollie suspected, to the barn.

Papa stirred, and Ollie offered him water. Her greatest fear at that moment was that he would wake up and fret about Ginna as she herself was fretting. She was afraid Papa could not withstand the worry. Thankfully, after she pulled up his quilts, he settled down to sleep quickly.

Ollie sat in the front parlor and tried to read her Bible. Her head was throbbing and her eyes stung in the dim light.

"Miss Ollie" she heard, after skimming at least half of the Psalms. At the top of the stairs, young Dr. Cummings summoned her calmly, "Could you bring some towels and water?"

"Sick, again? Is she…" but the door had closed quietly.

When Ollie brought the towels and a large jug of water, she tried to see into Ginna's room but Cummings thwarted her attempt to stick her head in the door. From downstairs, she could hear the voices of the strained voices of the two doctors and regular moaning from her sister. She was truly sick this time.

"Dear God, forgive me for accusing my sister of vanity and selfishness. Please heal her and restore her to us" she prayed.

Over the subsequent years, Ollie would try to reconstruct that night and the next day. Had she heard one of the doctors say to the other a word like "animale" or "a Molly?" What would that have meant?

Near dawn, Ollie straightened herself up on the settee where she had fallen asleep. Dr. Thorpe had come into the parlor and was standing in front of her.

"Who is the father?" he asked.

"Papa is still asleep but he was quite well yesterday. Ginna…"

"Ollie, I mean who is the father of the poor little baby that Virginia just delivered?"

Ollie felt like a mallet had been struck into her skull like a pig at killing time.

"She won't say. Insists she did not know she was in that condition and that she doesn't know how it could have come about." Dr. Thorpe's voice was ragged with fatigue.

"I can't begin to understand what you are saying. Ginna gave birth?"

"You hadn't noticed any changes in her?"

"Heavens, no. Just that she seemed to be getting more and more skittery every day. I was afraid she was going to be having another spell of exhaustion. This can't be. Ginna isn't married or even…"

"I doubt the child will live. It was premature and there are many problems. Your father will have to know and decide what should be done. As soon as he is up, please feed him something and let me talk to him in private. I know his health is frail but there is no other way but to have him in control of the next steps."

"I need to see Ginna."

"She is asleep and Andrew is trying to help the infant. I need you to see to your father right away…please."

When Ollie tried to stand, the effects of spending the night without taking off her corset or even putting her feet up, caused her to sway slightly. The doctor steadied her, and she went out to the kitchen to light the stove.

So as not to startle Captain Graham, Dr. Thorpe waited in the parlor until the old gentleman had eaten his breakfast. Then Ollie quietly told him that the doctor was here and needed to speak to him. The doctor closed the parlor door, and Ollie went to the outhouse and threw up. She walked out to the barn where she found Stuart asleep on two hay bales, a bottle on the floor next to him. She sat down on another bale and watched him sleep. When he woke up, instead of her usual lecture, she simply said, "God help us, Stuart."

The two made their way to the house after Ollie had presented the scant information she had to Stuart. Her brother had not expressed shock. He had simply shaken his head and said, "Always Ginna."

The parlor door was now open and Papa was being assisted up the steps by Dr. Cummings. All was oddly silent in the big old house. Within a few minutes, Ollie and Stuart could hear their father's voice. Strangely, he sounded as he might have ten years ago, full of authority and even vigor. Dr. Thorpe's softer voice broke in from time to time and then keening, not sobbing, from Ginna. Where was the baby? Was it dead? Didn't newborn babies cry?

Stuart hurried to get his face washed and change his shirt. Ollie tried to drink a cup of coffee but could not swallow. After what seemed like hours, Dr. Cummings came down and asked the two of them to join their father and sister. To their surprise, when they reached the top of the stairs, the young doctor did not go into Ginna's room but across the hall to the boys' old bedroom. Ollie glanced all around the sickroom to try to see anything that looked like a baby. When her eyes rested on Ginna, she was appalled. Her sister looked worse than the corpse of their dear friend Della, who had recently succumbed to tuberculosis. She longed to smooth Ginna's sweat soaked hair and put a clean gown on her but mostly to comfort her obvious terror.

"Stuart, Olivine, the doctors and I have agreed that this day will never be mentioned. I am sure you understand that our family sets a standard in this valley, and we cannot allow Virginia's error, the result of her nervous illness, to become an object of gossip among those who might enjoy an opportunity to look down on us."

What would they do, Ollie wondered? Bury the little body in the old graveyard their ancestors had used before the Grahams took to committing their bodies to the church cemetery?

Outside of that dilemma there was no reason for anyone to

know.

"Dr. Cummings will take the child to the orphanage in

Lynchburg by train this afternoon. It is my expectation that

Hayden will do the honorable thing and marry Virginia as soon

as possible."

Hayden! Stuart and Ollie quickly glanced at each other

incredulously

So the baby, was still living and able to travel to Lynchburg.

That was a blessing, Ollie couldn't help but feel. Then a wave

of sadness swept over her and she ran from the room. She did

not attempt to enter the bedroom where Dr. Cummings and the

baby were. She knew she couldn't bear to see him once and

then never again. How strange that with all the nieces and

nephews Carrie had provided for them, it was this poor little

fellow that felt like her own being taken away.

For the next few days, Ollie and Stuart tiptoed around their

father, who continued to seem to have renewed energy and

health in spite of the horror that had transpired. Hayden
appeared at the house two days later and, with the minister and
the two siblings as witnesses, Ginna and Hayden were married
in the bedroom. Thank the good Lord it was winter and not
many folks were out and about to visit and gossip. The marriage
was simply announced from the pulpit at church the following
Sunday.

People stayed away. No one was bold enough to approach the
Grahams' doorstep except for Hayden Graham, the bridegroom,
who called in daily and sat by Ginna's bedside, holding her hand
and talking to her of pleasant things though she did not respond.
Captain Graham, his cousin and now father-in-law, greeted him
each day at the door and bid him good-bye as if it were the most
normal circumstance in the world.

Meanwhile, Clayton Hill was on fire with speculation. Birdie
and William Maples' daughter had been born the very same day
as Ginna's infant. For the rest of her life Kathryn Maples would
be reminded that her arrival had been overshadowed by what
happened at Captain Graham's. All kind of wild tales were

proposed. Some ardently denied the rumor that Ginna had given birth, saying it was beyond belief that a lady from that family would stray so far beyond the bounds of convention. Others would counter that Virginia has always had that odd turn to her. "You should hear about her great aunt Maribelle and the cousin in Danville. Shameful."

One old-timer cracked that the consumption of firewood in Clayton Hill was greatly diminished by the sheer heat of the gossip going around. Gossip about whether there had been a birth and, if not, why the sudden marriage, swirled only until it was completely engulfed by what happened 5 days later. On the 11th, Ollie got up shortly before daylight to be sure her father would not have to wait on his breakfast. Though Ollie had cried in secret, Stuart was making himself scarcer than ever, and Ginna was virtually speechless, their father continued to be blessed with good spirits. Ollie almost believed that the restoration of his health was the recompense they received for the blow dealt by what had happened. Papa's prayers at the table were the most eloquent he had made since before their mother died. Ollie suspected that even Stuart was stirred.

It was after 7:30, and Papa had still not made a sound. Ollie told herself she would wait another ten minutes before starting his eggs. The biscuits were already getting cold. She waited for five minutes and, finding herself suddenly too anxious to wait another second, she crossed the hall and tapped on her father's door. Sometimes he did linger on the commode they had insisted he use rather than going out in the weather to the toilet.

"Papa, dear, are you awake?" When she received no answer, she knocked on the door again and then pushed it open. The shocking sight of her father, his pants around his ankles, his mouth agape, his head fallen back and to the right, eyes seeming to accuse her of defiling his privacy, made Ollie scream and scream. Stuart appeared behind her and covered his father with a quilt, then carried his lifeless body to the bed.

The funeral took place the next day, and all of Clayton Hill showed up in the church yard to see who would be at the burying. Looking fragile as a willow switch, Ginna stood supported between her new husband and her sister. Their two brothers and older sisters resolutely showed no emotion, as Papa would wish, carrying on at any time, especially a funeral, being considered common. The other attendees, having studied the faces of the Graham family, knew that any information about what had transpired in that household in the past week would be concealed as thoroughly as the remains being placed in the grave. For the next two generations in Clayton Hill, however, theories and counter-theories bred like mice.

Part II

"In these circumstances they did what most of us do, and, being ignorant of the truth, persuaded themselves into believing what they wished to believe."

— **Arrian**, *The Campaigns of Alexander*

1883 Marriage
Stokes Gap, Tennessee

Stokes Gap in the extreme northeastern corner of Tennessee, wedged between the ancient mountains of North Carolina and Virginia, is noted neither for the richness of its soil nor the warmth of its hospitality. Families who choose to stay there generation after generation tend to like their own company and not too much of even that.

One such family was the Cummingses, antecedents of young Dr. Andrew Cummings. In 1883, John Cummings had brought his bride, the former Ada Teegarden, to live in the small community of Stokes Gap, on the family farm he had inherited from his father. John Cummings was jumping into adulthood with both feet. In addition to bravely attempting to make something of the farm, he had also opened a medical practice the prior year. It seemed to him fitting that he complete the transition by establishing a marriage.

John had been a small child during the Civil War. His own
father had been too old to fight, but was known for his
contrariness. John was the youngest child in the family and,
because he excelled in school, the only one who received a
higher education.

Ada was a first-year student at Peabody Normal School in
Nashville when John visited his old friend, Nathan Teegarden, a
cousin of Ada with whom she was boarding. John was instantly
attracted to the slightly dreamy intelligence and innocence he
saw in Ada. After their first meeting, they corresponded
regularly for six months. When John returned to Nashville in
the late spring, he proposed, and they married two weeks later.

A teaching career had been the idea of Ada's widowed mother
and her two older brothers. Ada's abandoning it relieved the
brothers of the financial responsibility for schooling and
deprived her mother of the hope that Ada would come to
Bowling Green and care for her. Mrs. Teegarden had lived in a

state of near poverty and perpetual mourning since the death of her husband, a Union veteran, shortly after the War, when Ada was quite small. The military affiliation of Mr. Teegarden was never spoken of except behind closed doors, though their hometown of Bowling Green, Kentucky, had been fairly equally divided between Northern and Southern sympathizers.

Ada felt no longing to return to the cramped and sad home of her childhood. On the other hand, she hadn't the dimmest idea of what life with John offered in exchange.

When the newlyweds arrived early one morning at the train station in Bristol, they were met by a small, shy-seeming boy of about 17. John simply said, "Ada, this is Ez."

The look of utter befuddlement that greeted Ada brought to her mind all the joking remarks her school friends had made about the hillbillies she was going to live among. Indeed, Ez said nothing when Ada said "Nice to meet you Ez." He gawked with his mouth slightly open, until John said, "Let's get our bags and get home. We've a long ride, and it'll be dark if we don't hurry."

Ez's family, the Allisons, had worked for the Cummingses since long before John was born. In fact, Ez's parents, both of whom had died within weeks of each other, had lived in a three-room cabin just yards from the main house. Now, Ez lived there alone and had been doing the work of a grown man since he turned 13. In truth, he knew much more about farming than the earnest John.

All that long, winding trip, Ada wondered at the scenery that presented itself. Once, she gasped at the sight of a waterfall as they rounded a curve in the rough road. Ez turned back from the front seat of the wagon to look at her. "What is that bird?" she asked John when she spotted a redwing blackbird. "Oh, what a beautiful place this is. You didn't tell me!" The further they progressed, the fewer houses they passed, though small cabins were spotted occasionally through the dense growth of the trees. Cornfields and tobacco fields became rarer as the wagon dipped into dark hollows before emerging into sparkling sun.

Exhausted as she was, Ada couldn't stop drinking in the sights that kept surprising her. John asked Ez questions about things on the farm. After all, this was the season between planting and harvesting, and prospects for success or failure were in the balance. Enough time had been spent on marrying, and traveling back home. John had business to get to.

Awkward attempts to master housewifery consumed Ada for the first several months in Stokes Gap. Having never been in a position to observe the dynamics of a marriage firsthand, she would not have said that she was disappointed in her role as Mrs. Cummings. It did sometimes occur to her, though, that she often heard more words in a day from the heretofore dumbstruck Ez than she did from her spouse. John was gone from early in the morning, and often during the night, on medical house calls. Though he did have a small office for seeing patients in a back room, that had a separate entrance, and she seldom encountered the patients.

Ada's only social outlet was with the ladies of the Stokes Gap Methodist Church where the Cummingses had worshiped for generations. Though she missed the comforting familiarity of the Episcopal Church back home, like most women of her class and time, Ada was convinced that Christian fellowship was the answer to her loneliness and that might be found in whatever church was at hand. The older women of the church, who had known her late mother-in-law, were gracious. However, what she at first took for friendliness from the women her own age turned out to be curiosity – curiosity about whom John Cummings had brought back from Nashville and what about her would have attracted him when none of the hometown girls could turn his head. After meetings Ada often found herself ruminating about what she had said and what had been said to her and how she might be more engaging next time. She never named her loneliness, even to herself.

To Ada's surprise, John had distanced himself from the church since his college days. He had done a lot of reading of scientific and philosophical writings that were inimical to the predominant thought of the day and region.

His particular interest was botany, and he spent most Sundays looking for rare specimens. He pursued the illusive Oconee Bell every spring.

Specimens of the plant had been found in the Carolinas and in Georgia. John was convinced that he had seen it in his native environs as a child, long before he knew its name. When he stumbled on the writings of Asa Gray, he became obsessed with confirming his recollection, an obsession that was to persist for the rest of his life.

Within three years, Ada gave birth to two sons. Any void in her marriage went unrecognized as she devoted herself to her babies. John seemed not to have noticed that the "dreaminess" that had attracted him to her had evaporated, along with the wit and charm which required the presence of friends to flourish. Mothering was exhausting for Ada, and John saw to it there were no more pregnancies after the boys were born.

Young Ez was often in and around the house, either working or talking. He teased and petted and entertained the little ones, cheering their mother as well. It had been a matter of consternation, and some amusement, that little Andrew, when he finally began to talk at age four, called both the men he saw every day, his father and the hired man, by the same name: *Ez*.

Andrew was quiet to the point of apparent backwardness. Before he was old enough to start school, Ada worried that he might be slow. John Cummings assured his wife that Andrew would turn out all right, just as he himself had done. Although he made excellent marks in school, Andrew was not especially favored by his teachers because of his lack of congeniality. Miss Teensy Crabtree, fourth grade teacher, had remarked to her colleagues that, "...sometimes that Andrew Cummings gives me the feeling he is studying me and finding me lacking. I wish he'd act like a normal young 'un once in a while."

Farley, on the other hand, with his freckles and red hair, was irresistibly charming to adults. An indifferent pupil, he managed to get away with a lot of mischief because of his attractiveness. His schoolmates knew better than to challenge Farley in disputes because he was tough as whit leather and sneaky. At home on the farm during their early years, the boys were forced to rely on each other for playmates even though their interests were different.

In spite of having withdrawn from the church, Dr. Cummings did adhere to at least one Biblical edict, Proverbs 13:24. Farley earned plenty of whippings and endured them stoically. Andrew was terrified of his father and gave him a wide berth. Andrew's punishments were usually the result of, not intentional misbehavior, but mishaps due to inattention or clumsiness.

"My earliest memories of Papa are of me hanging on my mama's skirts, trying to hide from him. He seemed 10 feet tall and made of stone," Andrew was to recall.

"I don't think medicine was his true calling though he made a good job of it. When he wasn't doctoring or supervising Ez on the farm, he dearly loved to go tramping around the creeks and hollows looking for rare plants. He kept a notebook in which he pressed examples. I remember him sitting up late at night working on it. The few times I ever saw him show what you'd call excitement were when he managed to locate one of those obscure species."

John seemed to display his warmest feelings for his horse, Galileo, a bay gelding, said to be smart as a human. The doctor would permit no one, even Ez, to curry and comb his horse. The boys shortened the horse's name to Leo, but Ez insisted on calling him Gal.

1894
Parthenia Comes to Stokes Gap

When the two Cummings boys were around eight and ten-years old, young Ez, who was by now a seasoned and essential hand on the farm, brought a bride home to the valley with him. Parthenia Mullins most likely never thought of herself as a bride. Several inches taller than Ez, as quiet as he was garrulous, lean and dark, she was a mysterious addition to the Cummings farm. Discreet questioning by Ada revealed only that Parthenia had come from "a right smart piece up yonder near Kentucky, up in Claiborne County." Ez stated he met her at the fair in Knoxville and claimed to know nothing about her family. This lack of information from Ez, who usually could not be hushed, frustrated the curious Ada to no end. Having another woman on the farm, no matter how different their backgrounds, just might provide her with a badly needed bit of female company.

Ada had no idea how to be someone's employer. Her hesitancy

to give orders to Parthenia proved frustrating and embarrassing for both of them for a while. Little by little, though, they began to develop a rhythm of communication regarding the housework. Beyond that, their awkwardness continued.

One day, after about two months on the farm, Parthenia approached Ada shyly. She confided that she did not know how to read or write and said she would, "most dearly be thanking you for the writing of a word" to let her family know how she was faring. The letter was brief, unedited by Ada.

Dear Mammy and Pap,
I pray the good Lord has took care of you since I come up here.
I married Ez Allison and help him on Dr. Cummings' farm in Stokes Gap. I hope I did not give you too much aggravation slipping off like I done.
Your daughter,
Parthenia Allison

The letter was addressed simply to "Jepro Mullins, Tipton

Tennessee." If Parthenia received a response, she did not mention it.

Parthenia followed Ez's example of interacting with Andrew and Farley to a degree, though she was more business-like. She taught them some of the realities of farm life that Ada was squeamish about: pig-killing, kitten drowning, chicken beheading, and rabbit skinning, for example. The boys were enthralled with her backwoods skills, not to mention her frequent use of Anglo-Saxon words which Ada pretended not to hear.

The two men, being opposite in temperament, supplied the women with occasional amusement. Dour John and babbling Ez were not aware that their wives had begun to form a bond based on exchanged glances and raised eyebrows at the idiosyncrasies of their men.

Unbeknownst to the guileless Ez, his talkativeness nearly set John's teeth on edge. It was beyond the doctor's comprehension how a man could talk so much and work so hard at the same time. In spite of the proximity of another doctor, who provided some competition for his medical practice, John was most often either seeing patients at his little office or making house calls. His dealings with the farm consisted mostly of overseeing and critiquing Ez's management. Because of Allison relatives all over the area, it was easy for Ez to recruit additional hands for haying, dipping sheep, and harvesting. Ez dreaded the days when Dr. John was free to actively participate in the farm work. On those days, he felt as if God were looking over his shoulder and that God was not as good a farmer as he thought He was.

The sheep were turned up into the mountain each spring after lambing. There they lived a mostly idyllic life, protected by two fierce collies, until the arrival of cold weather in late fall. A few weeks after the first frost, Ez and whoever his current helper might be, would go up into the mountain and herd the ewes and their lambs back down into the fold. Some would be taken to market and others kept on for another season. In Ez's estimation, this sheep venture, begun on a whim by Dr. John several years back, was a losing proposition. Many were lost to the wolves, in spite of the dogs, and the market for wool was depressed. The labor involved in maintaining Doc's experiment did not seem justified to Ez. He had not refrained from expressing his opinion to his employer on numerous occasions. One November, before the end of the old century, all the sheep had been brought to fold except for one balky ewe. The weather turned abruptly on the 13th and snow was beginning to fall heavily. Dr. Cummings kept insisting that Ez go fetch that last ewe. Ez kept making excuses. Ada and Parthenia sensed a building tension that might, for a change, turn into an open disagreement that could spell an end to their satisfactory arrangement.

John said, "Ez, I am telling you once and for all, go get that ewe before she is lost to me. No more of your damned stalling."

"Doc, how much you reckon she'd fetch at market?" Ez queried.

"Prices aren't much this year but she has produced some mighty pretty, fat lambs the last three springs."

"Yes, sir, she has. How much you reckon she'd fetch?"

Feeling certain that either a stroke or indictment for homicide were in his immediate future, John replied through clenched teeth, "Probably not more than $4 or $5 this time of year."

Ez reached into his coat pocket for his worn change purse. He counted out three dollar bills and two dollars in change, most of his pay for the first two weeks of the month. "Let her lay where she be," he said, handing the money to the doctor and walking out the kitchen door.

John encouraged Ada to spend more time with the church women, though he avoided the company of their husbands. He did not realize that the stringy, illiterate wife of his farmhand had gradually begun providing her with more camaraderie than she had experienced since girlhood.

Grateful as she was for Parthenia's practical wisdom in certain matters, Ada knew that there was one sort of experience Parthenia lacked. Ada liked to imagine the time when she would confidentially advise her about being in the family way and taking care of a newborn. She knew how strong Parthenia was but reasoned that any woman the guidance of another when that happens for the first time. Having a doctor for a husband, she recalled, had in no way made up for absence of a caring female. Of course, the subject was never brought up in conversation between the two of them but Ada knew that the day would come when Parthenia would run from the kitchen retching or need to sit down for a moment or crave starch.

One winter morning after Parthenia had been there for a year or so, the two women were washing in the wringer washer on the back porch. They had the cook stove heated up to warm the kitchen, where they would drape the wash over the drying racks and chairs and safes. Parthenia was unusually talkative and had been shyly recounting to Ada a story of Ez's courtship. As she laughed at herself, she tugged on a sheet as it came through the wringer. Ada was opening her mouth to ask about a particular of Ez's wooing when the expression on Parthenia's face dissolved. She kept tugging on the sheet as a pool of blood formed at her feet. The she bent her head over and leaned on the washer.

"I am so sorry, Mrs. Cummings. It's happening again. They just don't take."

Shocked and frightened, Ada thought there must be some womanly wisdom or help she could offer. "Let's get you stretched out on the sofa. I'll try to get hold of John. He'll know what to do."

"No, I'll just go up to the cabin and let the rest of it pass and get cleaned up, like always. Maybe you can get this last sheet out and I can do the ironing tomorrow? If you'll just bundle up the other stuff when it's not hard dry and leave it out here on the porch, it'll do just right for ironing in the morning."

It was Ada who began to cry in the face of Parthenia's loss. The miscarriages and stillbirths continued, as far as Ada knew, on a regular basis for the next decade or more until at long last Parthenia was to have her Ella Rose. Throughout those years,

Parthenia and Ez continued to dote on the two Cummings boys, especially Farley, while they longed and prayed for a child of their own.

A near tragedy with the horse showed Andrew something about the relationship between his father and Ez. The much bandied intelligence of Leo was evidenced in his knack for unlatching gates and stall doors. One evening, Ez had brought in the workhorses, Ned and Flossie, and fed them their sweet feed, which they had definitely earned pulling the plow all day. Leo didn't get much, if any grain when there was good pasture because he was not nearly as active. But he was jealous of the work team's repast, so he opened their stall doors right after Ez left to go to the cabin for his own supper. Leo sneaked in and ate every bite of the sweet feed intended for his two hardworking and weary companions.

No one noticed until early the next morning when Ez found all three horses in the barn lot. The minute he saw Leo pacing and sweating, Ez knew what had happened. He put Ned and Flossie in the barn and started walking Leo. Walked him all day long. Leo's bowel was twisted from overeating. In those days there weren't any veterinarians in that part of the country so each farmer doctored his own stock the best he could.

Unaware of the drama, John had left very early, before daylight. Later, Andrew and Farley hung on the fence, mesmerized by the suffering of the horse and by Ez's talking to him, and they were truly shocked to see the tears coursing down Ez's face. Soon, Parthenia brought water and a couple of biscuits to Ez and shewed the boys into the house.

John took over the walking when he returned from town. He never blamed Ez for what had happened. They took turns walking Leo all night long and smacked each other's backs when it finally became apparent that Leo was recovering.

After Leo died, years later, John never wanted another horse. The grief surrounding losing him was too wide to overcome.

1897-1902

<u>Excerpts from Letters of Ada Cummings to Her Mother</u>

March 3 1897

Dearest Mother,

I do hope to hear that you are recovering from the awful sickness you described in your last letter. Do you seem to be able to sit up longer and walk a bit?

The weather here has been exactly what one would expect of late winter in the mountains. John and Ez have struggled to feed the cattle and sheep and pigs, with snow every few days and gloom in between. The boys have been cooped up so long....since Christmas it seems. Of course, Andrew doesn't much notice. He would rather read than anything else anyway! Farley, you can imagine, is chomping at the bit for spring to come. He has gotten into some scrapes at school, resulting in notes home from the teacher. I know his naughtiness comes from lack of exercise and high spirits. His father does punish him for these transgressions at school, but I can hardly keep a straight face at that little imp's shenanigans.

We struggled to church Sunday, only to find that the service was canceled due to the weather. Rev. Lyons said he did not want the elderly trying to get out on the snow and ice but several had gotten out to no avail. There was a good bit of grumbling directed at the minister's decision, with some even asserting that he just wanted a day off.

I hope you will try to visit us this summer. If you are not able to, I will come to you in October as usual.

Forgive the brevity of this note. I am late to get started on my baking.

Your own,

Ada

January 2, 1900

Happy New Century, Mother! I feel sure that you, like John and I, were not awake to welcome in the new age. I can't say I've noticed anything much changed. The boys are over the moon about entering into the "future" as they call it.

Little news from here except to express thanks for the lovely Christmas gifts. I am perfectly delighted with my sewing kit. It is pretty enough to sit on the table next to me in the front room while we have guests....not that we have many. Farley's friends are often about the place, but the rest of us are relatively reclusive. Andrew is just a little old man before his time.

Of course, as you know from your visits, Ez and Parthenia are in and out daily. They provide me with more news of the outside world than does John. I don't know how they are able to pick up every bit of gossip, conveyed as essential bits

of knowledge, that floats around the town and countryside.
Sad to say, once again Parthenia was not able to carry her
child to term, though she certainly managed to get further
along this time. I don't know how she is able to be back on
her feet in a day or two, never shedding a tear that I can see.
John says she is made of stern stock with the exception of her
regenerative capabilities. He believes she will never succeed in
bearing a living child.

I nearly forgot to tell you that we had a visit at Christmastime
from a cousin of John's, Guthrie Abernathy. Guthrie is
John's mother's brother's son. He grew up near here and had
come from his home in Charlotte to visit some of the
relatives. Although they said they were childhood playmates,
if any man could be said to be John's opposite, it would be
Guthrie Abernathy. He is short, heavyset and jovial. I am
sorry to say he told some stories I would have preferred the
boys not hear. John soon tired of Guthrie's tales and found

the need to go to the barn to check on the horse. Farley was punished severely the next day for repeating some of Guthrie's more outrageous language to Ez, though Ez tried his best to provide an excuse for the boy.

Did you have visits from my nieces and nephews for the holiday? It is hard for me to believe that they are nearly grown. I pray they are all well.

I am planning to sew two or three dresses for spring from the pretty stuff I bought in Bowling Green last fall. If I am not mistaken, I may have enough for only two since I have been overindulging in mincemeat and candied pears!

Longing to hear from you soon that you are well and in good spirits.

Your Ada

May 13, 1902

Dear Mother,

School is drawing to a close. Simply impossible to believe that Andrew will be leaving for college in September. I have no concerns about his academic abilities but do worry that he will be lonely if he doesn't open himself up a bit to be less backward. I am thankful to say he has not experienced any more spells of asthma after the terrible fright he gave us last summer. Up until very recently, Andrew seemed as excited as I've ever seen him, anticipating the big step forward in his independence, but lately he has turned glum and peevish. Maybe he is realizing he will miss his family after all!

John has come up with a plan to keep Farley occupied during summer vacation in hopes of curbing some of his boyish mischievousness. If the plan (of farm work mostly) succeeds, Farley will build muscles and his parents will have fewer headaches!

We understand that you feel you are past traveling at this point in your life. Sad as we are not to be able to anticipate your visits, I will make plans to come to you once Andrew is settled in college and Farley in school in the fall. John says he may even come with me, if he can be assured of Parthenia and Ez supervising Farley while we are gone. I wish John were not so worried about Farley, but he is right in thinking Ez might let Farley sweet talk him into most anything.

The tulip bulbs I brought home last fall from your garden produced a riot of color last month. I took an arrangement of them and my hyacinths to church and received many compliments. The irises will need to be divided soon. Maybe a job for Farley? Dare I risk it? Maybe just a few of them to see how precise he can be. This is not part of John's plan!

I know you look forward to your visit from Aunt Edna. Please give her my best regards.

With love,

Ada

1925
<u>Recollections of Farley Cummings</u>
As Told To a Female Companion in a St. Louis Missouri Speakeasy

Farley's perspective of those years was quite different from his mother's. He was fond of recounting the following version to anyone who would listen for the price of a drink:

"I wouldn't go back to that place for all the money in the world. My folks threw me out when I was no more than a kid. They thought more of their damned puddinhead farmhand than they did of me. My brother, the esteemed doctor, he don't even know where I am.

Andrew was perfect in their eyes. I reckon he never made a low mark on any of his school work. He didn't have any friends, except he mooched mine. They couldn't stand him, thought he was a sissie. He was! Every time we would get up a little fun, there would be Andrew with his long face, saying "you'll get into trouble" or "are you sure you should try that?"

"One time, we had decided to catch one of the little pigs and put it in a box and leave it on the teacher's front porch in the middle of the night. Andrew kept fretting about the sow getting after one of us. A sow can kill a man over her piglets you know? Anyway, there were three or four of us getting all excited about this plan like young boys will do. I could tell Andrew was nervous as a cat. It would have been fine if he just hadn't known about it, if he'd been in the house studying his lessons or something, but no, he had to hang around pestering us. Finally, he said something like, "I can't let y'all do this; it's too risky."

"Let us?" I said. Well, we all set on him, grabbing him by the arms and legs and carrying him like the pig he was trying to protect us from. Funny thing is he didn't holler or fight; he just kept talking to us like we were little kids.

"Lock him in the granary," I yelled. It was just a little old shed built up off the ground with two big bins for grain. When you opened the door to it, you could see the dust from the grain floating in the air so thick you could hardly breathe. I jumped in one bin and started scooping a hole in the middle of it, making more dust fly till I was almost choking. It took all our strength to haul him up and over into the bin, and he still wasn't fighting. Ha. We stuck old Andrew's head down in that hole and started shoveling grain with our hands till he was covered up to his middle with his arms and legs splayed out like a gigged frog. Then he did start fighting and kicking but he seemed pretty well stuck. We took off running and laughing and coughing."

"Well, we had pretty much forgotten about the pig plan and were hotfooting it down to the springhouse when we saw Ez coming toward the shed. Ez is the simple-minded clod that worked on the farm. I got to laughing picturing how funny Andrew would look coming out of the shed with grain and husks in his hair and dust coming out of his ears so I told the boys we should get up on top of the hill so we could watch the show from a distance".

"Seemed like it took a long time for us to catch our breath and quit laughing. We kept watching for Andrew to come out of the shed. Ez had a bucket so I knew he was going in for some feed. Next thing I heard was Ez yelling, "God's sake, help me Farley, Thenie, somebody." He was dragging Andrew by the arms and laid him down real rough on the ground right outside the shed. I told the boys they better head home and I ran down to the shed and acted surprised to see Andrew lying there. I *was* surprised. He looked like hell. His face was blue. Ez turned him onto his side and was beating on his back.

"I was scared shitless; I'll tell you the truth. In a few minutes, Andrew started coughing and then his face got red and he threw up and threw up and threw up. Ez said, "Run to the house and get some water and a rag, and your mama."

"Parthenia, Mama, Andrew fell into the grain bin and got sick. Bring some water and a rag, Ez says," I yelled into the kitchen before running back to the shed.

When I got there, Andrew was looking real pale and staring straight ahead. Ez couldn't help himself from pestering him with questions. Andrew was not saying anything.

"You all right, buddy?" I asked. Andrew turned his eyes to me but never said a word. By that time the women were fussing over him. Mama also kept asking what happened. After while, they helped Andrew up to all fours and then to his feet and took him on into the house.

When they were gone, Ez looked at me and said, "I don't rightly know what happened but I reckon that you and that gang of boys has done something to your brother that you should be shamed about. Don't tell me, and I won't tell your daddy. You will have to study up some kind of way to explain it to your daddy that won't make it look like what it was. I ain't smart enough to help you on that and wouldn't if I could. Lord's looking after you and Andrew today because I think he'd have died if I hadn't been coming out here to get feed. You need to settle up with your daddy and the Lord, son."

Ez was right about one thing. I spent the rest of the day trying to think up a way to answer questions about how all this came about. As it turned out, I didn't have to because Andrew never would tell, and I sure as hell wasn't going to. I think Mama and Thenie kind of covered it up a little bit too, saying he must have had an asthma spell or something while he was hiding in the shed. Daddy checked him over when he got home but didn't say much. He almost acted like he thought Andrew was being a pantywaist too.

So that's one story about how I disappointed my forebears, sugar pie. Ain't I a rascal? Let me pour you a fresh one.

1902-1909
Secrets

As an adult, Andrew could not have told you when he and Farley became aware of Ez's secret stash of moonshine in the barn. Much like John's quest for the Oconee Bell, their mother's sick headaches, and Parthenia's female trouble, it was considered grown-up business, not mentioned overtly or investigated.

Andrew later believed he connected some of Ez's availing himself of the 'shine with Parthenia's miscarriages or spats between the two of them. He remembered Parthenia going nearly silent for a few days and supposed that was her way of showing Ez her disappointment in him. The mood would permeate the household, and all of them would avoid getting Parthenia stirred up.

By the time he was half-way through high school, Andrew knew he wanted to become a doctor, though he did not tell anyone. He was studious and lonely, but he focused his attention toward going to college and then medical school. Gaining entrance to a men's college in the eastern part of Virginia was assured, based on his excellent marks. He liked to picture himself as a serious student having the circle of friends that he lacked in Stokes Gap. Most nights as he tried to go to sleep, he constructed a fantasy of college life and, later, possibly a career as a beloved doctor.

For reasons he did not understand, even as an adult, he failed to acknowledge to himself the one, huge flaw in his plan. Andrew never stayed overnight with friends, as Farley did. He had literally never slept in a bed other than his own. His bed was equipped with an elaborate system of rubber sheeting, attended to, but never mentioned, by his mother, Parthenia, or Andrew himself. It was as familiar as biscuits for breakfast. One night in the spring of his senior year of high school, with his college acceptance letter reverentially placed square in the center of his desk, he awoke in a cold sweat. He couldn't go to college. He wet the bed, had done so nearly every night of his life. His father had tried a few concoctions guaranteed to cure the problem to no avail. The terrible night this realization hit Andrew led to weeks of the deepest misery he had ever experienced. His parents noticed that he abruptly stopped talking about college. He would change the subject when anyone else mentioned it. He hardly ate. He couldn't sleep because he dreaded waking up to soaked pajamas. Even his perfectionist attitude toward his school work declined.

"I think Andrew is feeling homesick before he has left home," Ada said to John. "I hope he won't decide against going."

"He doesn't have that decision to make. He's going. You baby him too much. He will be all right once he makes up his mind that a man has to leave home sooner or later."

"Well, the clothes I have been getting ready for him to take are not going to fit because he's getting so thin. Maybe he is ill."
"Not ill. He has never had to deal with anything the least bit difficult. I guarantee you that he'll have matured a great deal by this time next year."

In spite of his flagging interest in school, Andrew was valedictorian of the Stokes Gap Class of 1903. About the time of graduation, he came up with a plan, his only hope, he told himself. With the money he got from his Grandmother Teegarden, he purchased two neckties, a new shaving brush and an alarm clock. He packed the ties away. He applied the shaving brush, lathered with his father's soap, to his barely noticeable whiskers and practiced shaving twice a week. He set the alarm clock for midnight and 3:00 a.m. every night for a week. In that week, he wet the bed only twice, both times between 3:00 and 7:30. He adjusted his schedule to wake himself up at midnight and 4:30 the second week and achieved perfect success. Only once in the month that followed did he backslide, and that was because he had neglected to set the clock.

In July, Andrew insisted on helping with haying, something his asthma had prevented him from doing in the past. His appetite recovered, and his scattered freckles turned into a tan. Once again, there was constant talk of the year ahead at Hampden

Sydney. In mid-August, the rubber sheeting was consigned to the attic.

Farley played sports all through school. Although somewhat smaller than average, he was fiercely competitive and used every technique, fair or foul, to win an advantage over an opponent. Parents weren't involved in young people's athletics in those days, but word would occasionally reach John that his son's behavior was "ungentlemanly." After what John considered an inexcusable transgression on the ball field when Farley was 16, he was forbidden to participate in sports for the rest of that year.

Hampden-Sydney College was considered a "gentleman's school." Having been established just before the Declaration of Independence was signed, it was located near in the Tidewater region of Virginia. Andrew Cummings arrived on campus feeling like a bumpkin in spite of the carefully planned and packed trunk of clothes that accompanied him. Quiet as he was, he became even more inhibited due to his mountain dialect, so different from the mellifluous words of his classmates. In the lecture halls, however, he was seldom required to speak and soon made favorable impressions on his professors with his written assignments.

Many of the professors had been officers in the Civil War. Coming from a part of the country that had been less invested in the "noble cause," Andrew was a bit surprised at how often the subject came up in lectures, regardless of the curriculum. When his Latin professor made reference to similarities between Caesar's battle tactics and those of General Lee, for example, Andrew began to see that, for many of these old fellows, their

Andrew eventually made friends with two or three students who, like him, were not from moneyed "southside" families and were more interested in academics than in the young ladies at Randolph Macon or the newly established Sweet Briar College. The group studied together and, once in a great while, managed to have a bit of fun. As his first trip home approached in December, he was feeling fairly pleased with himself overall. He had withstood homesickness and the stigma of his wardrobe and accent and was doing well in his classes.

Unfortunately, the atmosphere back home in Stokes Gap was totally lacking in the congeniality Andrew anticipated. His father greeted him with a solemn handshake, and Ada managed a smile and a half-hearted embrace. Andrew looked from one to the other and then to Parthenia who stood near the sink with her arms crossed over her belly. "Merry Christmas," Parthenia finally mumbled.

Deeply disappointed and bewildered, Andrew had the awful sensation that he might cry. What a let-down. He'd imagined returning, if not in triumph, at least not to this tepid reception. He went up to his room to unpack his things. Soon, his mother appeared at the door. She stepped inside. "How glad we are to have you home dear."

"*Glad* wouldn't be the word I would use to describe the mood around here. Is there something I should know about?"
"Parthenia, is she sick again?"

"No, it's not Parthenia and it's not Ez, exactly. Farley...."

"Say, where is Farley? I expected him to be here spreading Christmas cheer. What's he doing, distributing mistletoe to the neighbors with young daughters?"

"Farley is down at Ez's. He is staying down there for a while."

"Lucky Ez and Thenie. What do you mean staying down there for a while.?"

"Seems Farley got into some mischief last week."

"Stop the presses! The little angel?"

"Oh, Andrew. It isn't funny. He got into something Ez had hidden in the barn."

"Ha, Ez's happy juice."

"You know....knew about that?"

"Mother, we've known about that for years. For that matter, we could always tell when Ez had indulged."

"Well, my word. I didn't know about it! You should have told me! Your father came upon Farley deathly sick in the middle of the night, and, when the truth came out, he told Farley that he could very well go live with Ez if that's the kind of life he wanted to lead. Ez took the blame and tried to convince John to bring the wretched boy back to his own bed but John would not hear of it. The worst part is that Farley seems to like living down there."

Farley did join the family for Christmas dinner, but had little to say and returned to the cabin early. For the rest of Andrew's holiday, the brothers had but one or two conversations, and nothing was said about the awkward living arrangements or what had precipitated them. John did not broach the subject either. What troubled Andrew the most about the situation was that John was so cold toward Ez, who comported himself like a penitent.

A few weeks after Andrew returned to college, he received a letter from his mother, saying, among other things, that Parthenia had indeed been "sick again" and, therefore, Farley was under the parental roof once more.

Andrew dutifully made his way through Latin, Greek, Mathematics, Biblical Studies, and English until, finally, in his sophomore year, he reached Physiology. From there on, though he passed all the humanities classes with at least a B, it was the sciences that provided him genuine enthusiasm.

His brother, in contrast, left college after one term. Although his parents would not discuss their concerns about Farley, Ez did mention at least once that it was past time for Farley to straighten up and fly right. Andrew could see that his parents were becoming middle-aged, with Ez and Parthenia not too far behind. The conversations he had with Farley during those years mostly consisted of Farley's boasting about romantic conquests and drinking.

Parthenia's history of frequent and abbreviated pregnancies was wearing her down. In her late 30's, having lost several teeth, she was looking much older. Ada prodded John to talk to Ez about avoiding further pregnancies. After resisting the idea of an awkward conversation with his hired man, the doctor, who was quite forthcoming with his patients about such matters, tired of listening to his wife's concerns and decided to broach the subject with Ez. He knew that Ada was right, but he had kept putting off the talk.

One night, attending a heifer trying to birth her first calf, the two men were alternating trying to turn the breech. John knew he wouldn't have to look Ez in the face while so occupied so he began a long, technical, cheerless monologue about the modern methods of preventing conception. As usual, the more uncomfortable John was, the more he talked and the more he explained and the more he relied on medical jargon. His lecture must have gone on for at least 15 minutes.

Finally, the little bull calf emerged and was turned over to his mama. Wiping his hands and arms on an old feed sack, Ez cleared his throat to respond. "Doc, Parthenia is way ahead of you on this one. She done figured out her own way. She has me sleeping on a pallet in the kitchen. That ought to work, don't you reckon?"

Apparently, this *did* work for some time, but Ez's drinking increased, as did Parthenia's stony silences. Ada, for one, especially missed Ez's joking and teasing.

By the time Andrew was entering medical school in 1905, Farley had gotten a job at the Stokes Gap bank as a teller and considered himself quite the "young man about town." There was conflict between him and John about Farley's use of the car. John had purchased a Model C Ford the previous year so he could more easily make house calls. Farley had lobbied for the Curved Dash Oldsmobile, but his father insisted the no-frills Ford was enough of a nod to modernity. Farley learned to operate it before John did. Ez was terrified of the machine.

If John was on his way out to a house call, he would give Farley a ride to the bank, or even let Farley drive it to the bank and then switch drivers. He would not, however, allow Farley to take the car when he was holding office hours at home. He never knew when he might be summoned to go to a patient. Farley was embarrassed to be seen walking, let alone being carried in the wagon by Ez, and kept up a steady campaign to convince his father to allow him to take the car, creating added tension in the household. Rarely, in the evening, Farley was allowed to use the car to go out to visit friends.

About three miles from the Cummings farm, in an area called Rocky Branch, lived a family of three, consisting of two daughters and their middle-aged mother. They had lived there for years with the mother's parents and brother, all now deceased. No one claimed to know how they supported themselves. They did have a bony cow and several chickens. Gladys Batts and her daughters very seldom appeared in town.

The older daughter, Bessie, was said to be "pleasantly plump". During the three years she had attended school, her teachers considered her slow. Susie was smaller and quiet with dark eyes and a habit of looking at people from their corners.

Ez had befriended the family and made occasional, furtive visits. Most men in the area knew about the ladies' hospitality. Many availed themselves of it. The house was very small, and just off the main room was a room called "the office." Beside the door to the office was a straight back chair. A man would place his hat in the sprung seat of the chair to indicate that the office was in use. Others would wait in the living room, nervously fiddling with their own hats. Married men would glance nervously at new arrivals, but mutually assured confidentiality was the rule.

As Ez was preparing to leave Gladys' company in the office one night, slipping money under the dresser scarf, he heard a man's voice in the living room. "Well, hello there, sweetness!" In a panic, Ez hoisted his suspenders and threw open the window. He put one leg through and, lying on his stomach, pivoted the other foot out over the short distance to the ground. He clutched the sill as he tried to steady himself for the drop. The old sill and apron began to crumble away in his hands, leaving splinters, which he was not to notice until much later. Gladys heard the cracking of the old wood, Ez saying "shit, oh shit," and the yelping of the deaf old dog whose tail Ez had landed on, then "aw oh goldang it."

The following morning being Sunday, Ez did not have more than the basic chores to do. This was a good thing because his left knee was swollen to the size of a small pumpkin, injured by the landing and aggravated by the long walk home in the dark the night before. He had managed to pick out the splinters by lamplight while Parthenia snored in her bed, but he was sore all over. He made his way to the outhouse and lowered himself to the seat with difficulty. There he spent a good bit of time, contemplating his folly. Rising was even more difficult, but he finally did so with a groan and a grunt. Emerging into the sunshine of that autumn morning, he beheld Farley leaning against a tree, his feet crossed, whistling and twirling Ez's hat on a forefinger.

"Suppose you'll be needing this when you go out visiting again, Ez?"

For the first time in Farley's life, Ez felt ready to kill him. The young smart ass was reveling in Ez's humiliation. Ez turned away from the realization and went into his cabin.

1909

Andrew and Farley

Ada was happy on the return trip from the graduation weekend. She knew John was proud of their older son as he finished medical school and embarked upon his future. She sensed the expectant energy in Andrew. He had been courting a girl from a very respectable family. Mae Foster would be the ideal mate for her son with her cultured manners and sense of ambition.

Ada allowed herself to daydream about a future in which Andrew would be married to Mae and practicing medicine in Richmond. If only they could all move to Richmond, maybe Farley would find a suitable woman and a good job and … but she knew John would never leave his beloved Stokes Gap, the farm, the search for the Oconee Bell, his horse, and all the rest of it. At least she could visit Andrew in Richmond often. That would be something to look forward to.

Arriving at the train station in the late afternoon, John and Ada looked around for Ez, or possibly Farley, to pick them up for the drive home. Ada thought of that ride so many years ago when she first came to Stokes Gap. Thank goodness the roads were better now, though they still had to ride in the buggy because the car was a two-seater. It was raining off and on, which would make the trip pretty miserable. The Cummingses went into the little depot to wait for someone to show up. As always, the train was late. John reasoned that Ez had been taking his usually Sunday rest and had failed to leave the farm on time, thinking he would still get there before the train did.

After about 35 minutes, John's patience was nearly exhausted. He even thought of the possibility of renting a wagon or buggy and starting out. Just as he was telling Ada that he was going across the street to talk to someone about such an arrangement, their neighbor, Oscar Mallory, appeared, wet from the rain and out of breath. "Doc, I am sorry I am late. By the time Farley hollered at me to come after you, it was too late to be on time."

"Well, we are grateful Oscar, but what's wrong with Ez and Farley? Why couldn't one of them come?"

"Farley's knee-deep in trying to clean up what's left of the barn, and I reckon Ez is on a toot."

"There was a cyclone?!" Ada asked, grabbing Oscar's arm.

"No ma'am. Barn burned."

"Lightening then. Come on. Let's get on the way so I can find out how bad it is," John said, picking up their valises and striding out into the rain toward Oscar's wagon.

Strangely, the three were mostly quiet on the ride. John did not ask questions, and Oscar was greatly relieved not to be put in a position to answer any. John did talk about his memories of that barn being built when he was a very small child and about the possibility of building a new one slightly further from the house.

Ada said, "Thank the Lord it was as far from the house as it was. We can afford to lose a barn, I guess."

When they pulled up into the yard, John jumped out of the wagon to join Farley at the ruins of the barn. Oscar took Ada and the luggage up to the house and dropped them off. Ada found Parthenia sitting at the kitchen table with a cup of coffee.

"What a welcome home! You all didn't want us to feel like we missed anything," Ada said as she set down her things. Parthenia's face looked hollowed out. "Oh, dear, has Ez taken the barn burning terribly hard? It's all right. We'll soon build another barn."

"Ez won't never get over what's happened."

"It was just a barn. No one was hurt. Poor Ez will sleep this off and be ready to get back at it come Monday."

"Mrs. Ada, it's the worst thing that's ever happened here."

Farley was raking through the remains of the barn, trying to pull out useable items. His father observed a degree of agitation he had never known Farley capable of. Before John could ask, words burst out of Farley, "It will be all right, Dad. It will be all right. I am sure Ez is sorry. He's so sorry he's been drunk since the fire happened. He knows what he's done. He said he knew you'd make him leave this time."

"What are you talking about Farley? What did Ez do?"

"I reckon he was up here enjoying his 'shine Saturday night and dropped a match. So drunk he didn't realize when he went back to the cabin. When I drove up and saw the barn on fire and hollered at him, he stumbled up the hill and almost fell down trying to figure out what to do. Then he went back to the cabin and got his gun and shot Leo. I was calling for him and Parthenia to grab buckets but he only saw to the horse."

"Galileo was in the barn?"

"Yes sir. He'd seemed a little lame on Friday, and Ez thought it

117

best to put him up so he could rest that right hind leg that gives him trouble you know."

John sat down on the blackened ground and put his head in his hands.

Farley worked into the night though there was little work to be done. Ez did not emerge from the cabin, and John didn't have the heart to confront him. Ada was frightened for John. On Monday afternoon, John drove into town to make a couple of house calls and to speak to his friends at the lumber yard about ordering materials for the new barn. When he returned to the car, opening the passenger door to place his bag on the front seat, he noticed an area on the door where the paint appeared bubbled. He had so many things on his mind that it didn't register immediately.

Back at the house, Farley was resting in his bedroom after his long night. Ada had unpacked their valises and was sitting at the table planning some meals and special desserts that she hoped might cheer up the household. Farley had not joined them at the table for breakfast or dinner. As far as she knew, he had just grabbed a bite of this or that between trips to the barnyard. He was taking the day off from his job at the bank.

John had two patients waiting at the little office when he returned at 3:00. Ada thought that getting back into his routine would be best for him. Around 6:00, after John had seen to his patients and gone out to walk around, beginning to stake out the area for the new barn, Ada began putting together their light supper. She went out to her flower bed to cut some peonies for the table.

John found Ez sitting on the cabin's front porch. Ez looked up as John approached and just shook his head and lowered his eyes to his lap. John sat down on the old straight back chair without a word. After some time, Ez said "Don't believe I felt this bad when Mam and Pap passed. Never grieved over anyone or anything like poor old Gal."

"I shoulda never put him up. He was the least bit lame on

Friday, and, Saturday, the cows got to running from heel flies, and he was running around with them. I thought I should put him up. Never should have put him up Doc."

Still, John said nothing. "You got to overlook Farley. He wouldn't hurt Gal for the world or let your barn burn down. I know he's heartsick."

"How did Farley let the barn burn?" John finally asked.

Then it was Ez's turn to be quiet for a very long time.

"Ez, how did Farley let the barn burn? I thought it was already on fire when he got home from town. He couldn't have done anything to stop it."

Ez finally looked up at John. He was casting about in his mind for an explanation that would exonerate Farley. "Well, uh, when he seen the barn was on fire, and he was trying to get the automobile started so it wouldn't catch fire, he, uh might have thought he let the barn burn?"

"Wait. Why would the car have been at the barn to catch fire if he was in town? What was the car doing near enough to the barn to be in any danger of burning?"

"Honest to God, Doc, I don't know. Me and Thenie had been down at Ruble and Gertie's all evening. We was walking back down the road real late, about 11, and that's when we seen the flames. I knowed it was too late to save the barn or poor old Gal so I just run and got my gun and seen Farley moving the car over in front of the house."

"I can't understand why the car would have been near the barn. What started the fire?"

"Don't know what started the fire. I reckon Farley and one of his friends had been at the barn."

"What in the hell would they have been doing at the barn that late and why would the car be there?"

Ez stayed quiet for another long minute. "Well, Doc, I reckon he liked to have the barn as a little, sort of, uh, quiet place to maybe play cards or such like."

"You are saying this was a regular practice?"

"I noticed from time to time that...I could tell they...some of them had been in there at night."

"More than playing cards?"

"Doing what young folks do, I figure."

Ada was bringing her flowers back into the kitchen to put in water. She noticed the outside door to the office was slightly ajar. John usually locked it from the inside when he finished office hours and came in through the dining room. She heard a cabinet door rattling and figured John had returned for something. Not wanting to startle him, she opened the door just wide enough to see inside. Farley was at the medical cabinet, sorting through some of the salves, she thought. She didn't disturb him, but returned to the kitchen.

As she set the table, her husband came through the kitchen door and pumped some water to wash his hands. Ada turned to smile at him encouragingly but could not get him to meet her gaze. She went to the foot of the stairs to call Farley to supper.

"Might still be asleep," John said.

"Oh, I thought I heard him up," Ada lied.

After a few minutes, Farley appeared, fully garbed in his work jacket and gloves. "I am going to go on out and see what I can get done before dark."

"Son, there's no more to do." John said. "Is there more to say?"

"No sir, I guess there isn't."

"Ez didn't start that fire, Farley. Ez doesn't smoke. You know as well as I do, he chews. They were over at Ruble's Saturday night."

"Well, then, I don't know how the fire got started. I just figured because of Ez's habit of going to the barn to get liquored up, that that's what happened. He's gotten worse and worse about laying up drunk every time something doesn't go his way. I don't know why you have put up with it all these years. I feel sorry for Thenie, and I know y'all care about them, but there's no excuse for Ez taking advantage of us like he does."

"Farley, Ez had nothing to do with that barn burning down. He feels terrible that he had to shoot Galileo to end his suffering. That's why he's been drunk for two days. Why can't you own up to being at the barn and, I don't know, something happened. You didn't mean for it to. I know that. How can you blame poor Ez for your own bad judgement?"

"I swear to God. I am your son, and you take his word over

mine? I never could do anything to suit you. I am sick to death of being treated like an idiot because I am not perfect like Andrew. You treat Ez and Parthenia like they were your blood, and you treat your own son like he doesn't have good sense. Goddamn Ez and Goddamn that horse and Goddamn you." Farley took off the gloves and threw them on the kitchen table, revealing heavily bandaged hands. He threw the jacket on the floor and turned to go back up the steps to his room, leaving his parents speechless.

Finally, Ada said, "Now, I understand what Parthenia meant. This *is* the worst thing that ever happened here." She began to sob.

Farley came down with a suitcase. "I am going to rent a room in town and go back to work tomorrow. Why don't you just go ahead and move those two in here so you can be one cozy little family?" He slammed the screen door as he left.

John heard that Farley returned to the bank the next day. On Thursday, he did not show up. He left the boarding house

without paying. At the train depot, they said he had bought a
ticket to Lexington, Kentucky, boarding early Thursday
morning. For days, then weeks, then months, Ada and John and
Ez and Parthenia waited for him to turn up and apologize or at
least send a letter but he never did. John was able to ascertain
that his small savings account at the bank still held $12.

At Christmastime that year, Andrew came on a brief visit from
his hospital training in Richmond. He brought with him a letter
he had received from Farley. Reluctantly, he shared it with the
family, though he knew it would break their hearts. The few
lines he felt compelled to read to his parents were…

*I don't expect ever to set foot in Stokes Gap again. Guess
I am just not good enough for the Cummingses...or even
for the Allisons come to that.*

*Tell them to act like I never existed, which, I am sure,
they would have preferred...*

The part he withheld was…

   ….just so you know I am still among the living, I am roaming around some out west, having a hell of a good time. The women out here aren't near so particular about who they give it up to. Every town seems to have more pretty young things than you can shake a stick at – and I have been doing a lot of shaking! I reckon you are heading for the altar, you fool. Congratulations, I guess.

John chose to tell Ez and Parthenia only that Andrew had heard from Farley, that he was well, but that they needn't expect him home any time soon. The new barn was in use, and Ez no longer had his hidey hole for moonshine. It didn't much matter, as he was no longer trying very hard to hide it. Though he managed to do his work starting early every morning, he now grabbed the jug from under his own front porch every evening. On some nights when he couldn't sleep and would walk around the farm,

John observed Ez bedded down on that same front porch.

For his part, John spent more and more of his time out on house calls. It briefly occurred to Ada that he might have a lover, but she couldn't summon the energy to care. Their infrequent conversations were of farm matters and the weather. Both of them, independently, had decided to tell friendly inquirers that Farley was happily settled out west, but John elected Kansas City while Ada offered Little Rock. No one was cruel enough to point out the discrepancy.

In April, Ada's mother passed away in Bowling Green. John went with Ada to the funeral, but Andrew was just beginning his year-long study under Dr. Thorpe in Clayton Hill VA and did not feel free to ask for several days off. Ada tried to soothe herself by imagining Andrew's wedding to Mae, planned for a year hence, but she most often felt herself to be in a fog like the ones they saw most spring and summer mornings on the mountain. She avoided thinking about Farley, but was aware that nothing, even her mother's death, seemed to have much impact on her.

One bright spot for John and Ada that summer of 1910 was the letters they received from Andrew. He was learning a lot from Dr. Thorpe and enjoying the small community they served. Although he didn't mention it, the attention of the eligible women flattered him. He had begun to describe certain patients and their ailments, without names of course, the medical aspects appealing to his father, and the character idiosyncrasies to his mother. His letters to Mae bore little similarity to the missives home, but both were, in their own way, love letters. Andrew could think of no other means to comfort his parents. He only wished that he had some way to do the same for Ez and Parthenia.

In September, Parthenia announced she was going to visit her kin, for the first time since her arrival in 1895. Noting the bulging carpetbag and Ez's glum expression, Ada hesitated to ask for details, but assured Parthenia that they would miss her and that she had certainly earned the holiday. She was taken aback when Parthenia then grabbed her hand and shook it vigorously, turning abruptly to descend the steps and climb into the wagon. John noticed that, after Parthenia's departure, Ez was even quieter than he had been since the barn fire and showed no signs of imbibing.

One day, out of nowhere, Ez said, "Doc, women are so durn peculiar. Well, I don't know. Maybe I am peculiar. A woman can drive you god darned crazy, but, when she's gone, and you study about it a while, you figure you are much more crazier without her."

John said, "Ez, I think we are all a little bit crazy. Put two crazy people together, and they will cancel each other out sometimes. Maybe that was the plan when Adam and Eve, or somebody, first came along. I'll tell you one thing: your Thenie is one of the best women that ever was, even if she tries to make you toe the line. If I were you, I'd be heading for Claiborne County with a rosebud in my teeth."

Sure enough, Parthenia was back home by October. Though John continued to spend more time out on house calls than previously, and Ada to spend more time in her bedroom, the four settled into a new routine, each carrying a private burden of grief. Farley's name was not mentioned. Photographs of him were wrapped in tissue paper and placed in the bottom drawer of Ada's dresser. When John happened to enter a room and find Ada quietly weeping, he turned and slipped silently away.

Part III

"What mortal is there of us, who would find his satisfaction enhanced by an opportunity of comparing the picture he presents to himself of his doings, with the picture they make on the mental retina of his neighbours? We are poor plants buoyed up by the air-vessels of our own conceit."

- George Elliot

1918
Ella Rose Allison and Julian Cummings on the Porch

The children were playing on the front porch. Ada Cummings and her pretty daughter-in-law Mae could hear them through the parlor windows as the two women talked of domestic concerns, the pantry moth problem and the change in ladies' fashions and their shared concern over the danger of Ada's son and Mae's husband, Andrew, working too hard.

"I can spell TENNESSEE," Ada's grandson, Julian said.

"I can spell SPECTROGRAPH," said Ella Rose Allison.

Julian was a very bright six-year-old, visiting his grandparents from Chattanooga. Ella Rose was about a year older and had lived her whole life on the Cummings farm.

"Can you count to100?" Julian asked.

"Can, and know my times tables up to the sixes!" Ella Rose replied.

"You do not. You don't even go to school yet!"

"I don't go to school because I am flicted, Mizzie and Momma say, and I am bright as a new penny. Do you even know what flicted means? It means I am extra special."

"Does not and you are not as smart as me," the little boy insisted.

"Am too."

"You are a cripple, and she is not <u>your</u> Mizzie. She is <u>my</u> Grandmother."

The women looked at each other. Ada rose to her feet. As she opened the screen door, she saw Ella Rose standing next to the porch railing and then heard Julian's whimpering. Mae followed her to the porch, calling for Julian as the whimpers turned to howls. Ella Rose only lifted her chin as the women looked over the railing and saw the boy upended in the barberry hedge.

"The little shitbird fell off the porch railing. I don't know how in the world it happened."

Parthenia, who had been ironing in the kitchen, came around from the backyard. She picked up Ella Rose, turned her over on her lap, pulled up the little girl's dress and gave her three sharp smacks on her drawers.

"Oh, Parthenia, don't punish her. The poor little thing," Ada protested.

"One fer hurting Julian, one fer cussing, and one fer bragging on herself. Now get off home, Miss Priss," Parthenia commanded, pointing up the dirt road to their cabin.

Ella Rose had not cried, and would not, in front of Julian. She straightened her dress with as much dignity as she could muster, raised her chin again, and hobbled down the steps and across the yard.

"I think Julian hurt her feelings, Parthenia, and his father will take care of him this evening" Mae said, when Ella Rose was out of earshot.

"Her feelings is gonna be hurt wherever she goes because of her affliction. That don't mean she can go pushing folks into bushes all her life," Parthenia replied as she turned and walked with her unbelievably long stride back to the kitchen.

Ada glanced over at her grandson as he inspected the scratches on his legs, "Julian, you go on over to Ella Rose's house and tell her you are sorry. You must never make fun of someone who has a deformity. Ella Rose is your friend."

Eager to resume their earlier adventures and convinced that his mother would "forget" to tell his father, Julian lit out after Ella Rose.

"Parthenia expects too much of that child. It's a miracle she is even alive, much less able to walk with her twisted little skeleton," Ada said to her daughter-in-law.

"Yes, but I am afraid that her momma is correct in thinking that folks will not be able to ignore her infirmity. Not just her walk but her face. I find it hard sometimes to look at the child myself," Mae admitted.

"What a bright mind, though! I can hardly keep up with teaching her the primary lessons, she goes ahead so fast. My gracious, when John lets her look at the Spectrograph pictures, she asks so many questions about them that even he is hard-pressed to come up with the answers. Parthenia is determined to send Ella Rose to school next year and I can't bear the thought of her being mistreated by the other children. Did I show you what the Jewel Tea man brought last week?"

1919-1923
Ella Rose Goes to School
Stokes Gap, Tennessee

To say that Ella Rose Allison thrived in school would be the grossest understatement. Within her first three years of school she was moved ahead by two terms. Her teachers loved her. They marveled at the gifts of this physically crippled child, especially considering her uneducated parents, Ez and Parthenia. All of them, however, were well acquainted with Ada Cummings, who, they were aware, had nurtured her in many ways since her birth.

Because she often completed her work ahead of the other pupils, Ella Rose spent the extra time reading any available book and improving her penmanship. At recess, she could not participate in Red Rover, hopscotch or jump rope, but she was counted upon to serve as referee. Years later, this demanding role was to play an important part in her career. None of the girls could best her at jacks. She had a pretty little bag for her jacks and ball, made by her mother, and a callous on the outside of her right hand from sweeping up the jacks in uncounted games. The other girls had to assist her down on the hard-packed dirt where they played, but once she was in position, she was a dogged competitor. Her friends included her in the game Pretty Girl Station and wanted her on their team because of her creative acting out of occupations.

When Ella Rose came down with a childhood illness such as measles, both Parthenia and Ada fussed over her equally, but there was disagreement as to how long she should stay home from school with a cold. Ada wanted to keep the child home, preferably at her home, for a week, while Parthenia did not believe in coddling. John was inclined to side with Parthenia.

It was decided by John and doctors in Bristol that a specially designed brace would be helpful to prevent further curvature of Ella Rose's spine. After a long, tiring procedure to measure for the device, plans were made for her to spend a week at the clinic during the summer after she turned 11 to be fitted and become adjusted to it.

"I will get us a room at the hotel," Ada proposed to Parthenia.

"Who is *us*?" John asked.

"Why, Parthenia and me," his wife responded.

"I don't need no room. I'll be staying with my girl," Parthenia announced with a stubborn set to her face.

"Oh, you will exhaust yourself. I thought we could take turnabout sitting with her. One could rest at the hotel, while the other one looks after her," Ada responded.

"Miz Ada, I ain't resting at no hotel. Ella Rose is gonna need her mam with her, and her mam is gonna be there."

"But, Parthenia, that's ridiculous. Why wear yourself out when the two of us could tend to her and not miss a thing the doctors have to say! I could read to her to keep her occupied."

Ez could see that his wife was beginning to bristle. John could see that his wife was *past* beginning to meddle.

"Ada, you and I can visit at least two or three times while she's there and take Ez with us. Having too many people hovering over a patient is the worst possible circumstance," John insisted, earning a furious look from Ada.

Ella Rose weathered the clinic stay well, with almost daily visits from her father and one or both of the Cummingses. Sadly, the brace did not provide noticeable results, and it later became necessary for her to use a cane to stabilize herself when walking or standing.

1924
The Bloom of Youth
Stokes Gap, Tennessee

"I am just worrying myself sick, Miz Ada," Parthenia confessed when Ada commented on her looking peaked one morning.

"Whatever about? You are not one to fret about anything I know of!"

"Been studying and studying and don't know what to do. Ever night I lie awake and toss and turn. It's that, lately, Ella Rose is sweet on one little old boy one week and then the next week on another."

"Well, good gracious, we don't want her settling on one at age thirteen, now do we?" Ada tried to make light of Parthenia's concern.

"Me and Ez knows and you know, Ella Rose ain't never going to be some feller's sweetheart. We know it. But she don't know it. She's got all them fairy tales in her head about the beautiful lady and the handsome prince and them living happily ever after and whatnot. I just can't stand thinking about her heart getting broke when it comes to her that them dreams cain't come true for her. I reckon she got to believing that one of them operations was gonna make her look like other girls."

Ada hadn't seen Parthenia so distraught since Farley left. "Oh, God love her. I always thought she was such a smart child and understood that she was different in a good way, never mind her handicaps. I guess all young girls think they will become the beautiful lady."

"We never carried her around on a satin pillow because of her being afflicted, taught her to stick up for herself. But, one of these days, some rascally boy, or even a girl, is gonna set her straight about how she looks to other folks."

"She is a favorite among her schoolmates, and when Julian and the girls come to visit us, they can't sit still until they run over to collect Ella Rose to play with. They think there is nobody like her."

"It's true, she's been blessed up to now but, when the sap starts rising in young folks, plenty of things can change along with their bodies. I remember lots of hateful remarks made to me on account of me being so tall and so plain, and that was from girls I'd knowed since we was weaned. I already knowed I was tall and plain, but it still wounded."

"Now you've got *me* worried sick. Must be some way to protect her from that sort of thing.
Has she...I've not seen any sign of...."

"The monthlies, you mean? No. I been aiming to getting around to talking to her about all that."

"'Better not waste any time. Maybe that would be a good time for us to have a talk with her and help her understand, in a most gentle way, what, hmmm, limitations she may face?"

"Her mam will have that talk with her," Parthenia declared, ending the conversation.

Parthenia did have the talk with Ella Rose about the monthlies but the other subject never came up. It didn't need to. Although Ella Rose never confided in anyone how or by whom her spirit had been broken, Parthenia and Ada, Ez and John all noticed that the light had gone out of her eyes. Ada spoke to Andrew about it when he was visiting. "What kid that age is not miserable? I wouldn't trust anyone who wasn't miserable at some point in their teens." Andrew tried to minimize concerns, but he observed Ella Rose carefully and worried that her physical ills might be accompanied by something worse.

"How are y'all doing?" Andrew asked Parthenia and Ez while sitting on the cabin porch late one evening when the children and other adults were up at his mother's house.

"Pretty fair, but Ella Rose has been awful sour these last months," Ez replied.

"Ain't sour. *I* get sour. Ella Rose is something else, don't know what," Parthenia corrected. "She don't hardly eat and goes off by herself to read ever chance she gets. Surprised she was willing to go up with Annette and Adaline to the house but they talked her into teaching them to play Rook. Dr. Cummings, I mean your daddy, done checked her, and she ain't got no fever nor nothing. She won't own up to being in any more pain than she was before this last operation."

"Probably will pass, but, listen, if her appetite gets worse or if she changes her behavior drastically, have Mother get in touch with me."

"You mean if she stops eating altogether or goes after one of us with a butcher knife?" Ez translated.

"Shut-up Ez," Parthenia snapped.

"Well, something of the kind, Ez. Sometimes young people start showing nervous problems around her age. We just don't want to let it get out of control."

Fortunately, over the next several months, Ella Rose's problems did not "get out of control." Her parents and the Cummingses noted that, though her reclusiveness did not get any worse, she did not return to her place as the spunky presence in their midst. When the Cummings children or others visited, her lack of enthusiasm for their company was apparent, even to the youngest, six-year-old Adaline. "Ella Rose, come on and play jacks with me. I won't cheat, I promise." The child sensed that because once, when she was five, she had been gently teased by Ella Rose about her determination to win a game, she was being punished. Why else would Ella Rose say no?

Both Annette and Adaline loved to brush and braid Ella Rose's long, beautiful auburn hair. They would unpin it and brush as many strokes as their little hands could manage and then take turns learning to braid. In the past, they had created elaborate hair arrangements, adding flowers, feathers, jewelry or whatever might come to hand, and then present their finished product to Julian and the adults for their approval. It was great fun for the little girls, and their "queen" had thoroughly enjoyed the ministrations of her attendants, but now she wouldn't sit still for it.

Ella Rose became especially ill at ease around Julian, her playmate and confidante since they were small. Being a boy, and, thus, behind Ella Rose in maturity, he did not realize that her self-consciousness was a result of her having been made painfully aware of her appearance. To Julian, she was the same old Ella Rose, his equal in everything except sports. As she seemed to put a damper on their friendship, he began to turn away from her. The turning away confirmed her suspicion that he found her repellent. In time, the connection between the children and their grandparents was affected because they were no longer as eager to visit.

Stokes Gap children entered high school at Johnson County High after completing seventh grade at the elementary school. Pupils from other schools were funneled in as well. Parthenia and Ada worried during the summer about what new hurts Ella Rose might face. They worried and they petted her and they complimented her until she was ready to scream, "I know what you two are doing! Just stop. I am not stupid. My body is crippled, not my mind." Of course, she said nothing but grimaced, which made them compliment her more. Parthenia made her several new dresses, hoping they would be sufficiently fashionable to make a good impression. Ada had helped her pick the styles and fabrics.

Girls, even in the remote mountains of Tennessee, were beginning to bob their hair. Mothers were horrified. The first thing Ella Rose noticed at JCHS was the number of girls with bobs. Her pinned-up tresses and dowdy homemade dress made her cringe in embarrassment as students greeted friends they had not seen all summer and began to gather in groups identified from their former school.

"Gosh, Ella Rose! I haven't seen you in ages. I am so glad to see a familiar face," a voice rose out of the crowd. Ella Rose turned to see Agnes Tindall, not a friend from her school but someone she had met at Epworth League gatherings. "I hope we have classes together. I don't even know where the rooms are. Hey, there's Billie Tate and she's bobbed her hair. Oh Lord. Come here Billie Jane."

From that first hour of the first day, about five girls formed an alliance that was to last throughout high school, and which insulated Ella Rose from much of the pain that her mother and her "Mizzie" had so dreaded. Only around these contemporaries did Ella Rose occasionally relax and show the side of herself that the family used to enjoy.

That year, Home Economics was introduced in many rural counties, including Johnson. When Ella Rose had told her parents she wanted to sign up for the class, Ez had said, "What in the hell do you need to go to school to learn about cooking and sewing? Your mam can teach you all that. You might as well stay at home." Parthenia was inclined to agree. School was for learning arithmetic, Latin, and science, subjects beyond their knowing.

"But, Pap, Home Economics really is a science. I will learn all about things like what's good for us and how to prepare healthy meals."

Parthenia snorted. "You ain't done too bad eating my beans and cornbread."

"Mam, I love what you cook. I just want to learn about sauces and souffle's like they eat in France."

Parthenia snorted again.

"Oh, and how to sew fancy clothes."

Ada thought that Ella Rose would benefit from learning these skills, especially the sewing, since she was likely to remain at home as an adult. It was decided that Home Economics could be fitted into Ella Rose's schedule as long as she continued to make good marks in her hard courses.

While a couple of the girls in her group became interested in boys and confided their romantic encounters, most were as limited in that sphere as Ella Rose. Agnes and Billie Jane, in particular, were studious and shy. Not that the three did not hang on every word of Nancy's description of a boy at the drugstore trying to get fresh with her. They would also talk about boys at school, who was cute and who was a dud, but Ella Rose had no illusions about claiming one for her own.

One evening during her sophomore year, while Ella Rose was up at the Cummingses' using their reference books for a history report, Parthenia was putting clothes away in the little room off the kitchen that had been converted from a back porch into Ella Rose's bedroom. Some of the girl's books and a notebook were on the bed. Parthenia never paid attention to these items because she could not read. Only picture books held any interest for her. This evening, though, she started flipping through the notebook. On the back few pages were scribbles, drawings of flowers, butterflies and hearts and what even Parthenia could make out as initials. E.R.A. and A.A. interwoven among the swirls and tendrils. Parthenia could spell her name and Ez's and

Ella Rose's so she knew what E.R.A. stood for but drew a blank on A.A. She closed the notebook and stacked up the books and began searching her mind for all the boys, and even men, she knew who might have those initials. This was difficult for her, but she did have a reasonably good idea of which names sounded like they started with A.

For days, Parthenia did her best to pursue the answer by asking questions of Ella Rose about who was in her classes, who was smartest, who came from this holler or that holler. Ella Rose became suspicious of her mother's sudden interest in her schoolmates.

"Leave the young'un alone, Thenie. Why don't you just go on over to the school house and get the principal to give you a list?" Ez suggested.

"Pishtt. I am just interested, that's all," Parthenia explained but she tried to curtail her obvious curiosity and use more subtle methods. She had gradually realized that her daughter was livelier than she had been for a year or two. This realization renewed her concern about Ella Rose having her heart broken again. If she was sweet on a boy, on A.A., it was bound to end up disappointing her.

Although Ella Rose encountered a little difficulty in Algebra-she made a B-high school proved to be much less daunting than her parents and mentors had feared. Her teachers seemed to like her, and all but the snootiest of the girls included her in their circles. A sharp but subtle sense of humor began to emerge as a way of shielding herself from too obvious curiosity about her condition.

Each spring, the high school held an open house for parents to meet the teachers and see where their children spent their days. The Home Economics classes prepared refreshments to be served in the front hall. The excitement of the open house was added to by anticipation of the soon-to-follow summer vacation, but it was also an opportunity for the students to dress up a bit and have a chance to show off for their parents and friends. Ella Rose was giddy with the prospect and had just completed sewing a new dress in her class. However, her anticipation was accompanied by a guilty conscience. Much as she loved her parents, she was at an age where she was painfully aware of their county ways and appearance, even in a setting as unsophisticated as Johnson County TN High School.

The evening of the open house, after a cold supper of ham biscuits and canned apples, the little family hurried off to the school. Parthenia wore her best dress and her best shoes, both older than her daughter. Ez had put on his newest pair of overalls and his slicked back hair looked like he had applied a bucket of lard to it. Ella Rose sensed that they were nervous about the occasion.

"Mam, you sure do look nice."

"Well, what about me? Don't I look pretty as Rudolph Valentine?" Ez asked. Ella Rose's stomach sank when she detected the smell of 'shine on his breath. Maybe he wouldn't get close enough to anyone for them to notice, she prayed.

Entering the school, she was greeted noisily by her friends, who were standing behind cloth-covered tables, setting out refreshments for the parents to have after they met with the teachers. Ella Rose joined them as quickly as she could, setting her parents free to mingle, to the extent they would in that unfamiliar setting. A stool had been placed next to the punch bowl, just high enough for Ella Rose to be able to get up on. She had practiced ladling for two weeks, perfecting the precise tipping of the wrist that assured the punch would arrive in the cup and not splatter back into the bowl.

Parthenia and Ez made their way through the classrooms using the directions their daughter had explained to them. Fortunately, Ez was, for the most part, too bashful to say much to the teachers as one after the other lauded Ella Rose's academic abilities. The last classroom on their route was Home Economics. When they squeezed past parents leaving the room, they were surprised to see that the teacher was hardly taller than Ella Rose, with dark, bobbed hair featuring spit curls. Her twinkling eyes and dimples made her look for all the world like a Kewpie doll.

"Now, you all must be the parents of my darling Ella Rose! I am so glad to meet you at last. I am Annabelle Armstrong," she bubbled.

Ez shook the hand she offered, while Parthenia stood speechlessly looking around the class room at everything except the teacher.

"You got a right smart of little old kitchens in here, don't you?" Ez said. "If that don't beat the bugs abiting! Our girl, she goes on and on about it. She's been trying out some of these receipts you been teaching her. Why, I am bound to say I sure have been eating good."

Parthenia said, "Ez, we got to get on back. Nice to meet you, Miss Armstrong." She had looped her arm through Ez's, a heretofore unknown gesture. She almost pulled him out into the hall and down to the refreshment table.

Ez talked all the way home. Ella Rose broke in from time to time to tell her parents something about the evening, which she regarded as a complete success. Parthenia said nothing.

1929

Ella Rose Ventures Out

John was strapping Ella Rose's trunk onto the back of the car. Because there was not room for 5 people plus Ella Rose's gear, Ez had volunteered to stay at home while the rest took Ella Rose to the train station to depart for Radford Teacher's College.

"Let me say bye to Pap. I'll be right back" Ella Rose said.

"Well, hurry up," her mother ordered.

Ella Rose was dressed in her second-best dress. You did not want to wear your best to travel. She made her way carefully down the path to the cabin. Ez was splitting wood for the stove. He did not turn around when she approached, though he heard her.

"I just wanted to tell you..." Ella Rose began.

"If any man ever told me a young'un of mine would graduate high school, much less go off to college, I would have called him damned liar to his face. Now you're going up to Radford to show them us Allisons got more between our ears than gristle. If that don't beat all," Ez said, only turning his head over his shoulder.

"Well, Pap, I'll be seeing you soon," she replied.

Ez turned his face toward her. It was contorted into an expression Ella Rose could not remember having seen. "We'll see you come Christmas," he whispered and turned back to the wood pile.

Once she settled into college, Ella Rose faced a serious dilemma. Of course, she was going to write home. The problem was, should she write to her parents and Doc and Mizzie all in one letter, or write to them separately. She knew that Parthenia and Ez would need help from Mizzie reading but she didn't want to hurt their feelings by addressing most of her remarks in a manner that would seem to communicate with the Cummingses. Finally, she decided to write two letters.

Radford Teachers College

Radford, Virginia

September 23, 1929

Dear Mam and Pap,

How are you? I am fine. The other students and the teachers are very

nice.

The classes do not seem like they are going to be real hard. I think I can

keep up with my work.

The food is not near as good as yours, Mam, but I am not likely to starve!

I go to the dining hall with two or three other girls from my hall.

We went to chapel on Sunday. It was not like church at home, but, as far

as I can tell, they were praying to the same God.

Please say hello to Mizzie and Doc for me. I will write again soon.

Your loving daughter,

Ella Rose

September 26, 1929

Dear Mizzie and Doc,

I have written to Mam and Pap, as you may know, so this letter is just for you. I have many exciting things to tell you, but doubtless will not be able to fit them all into one letter!

The classes seem easy so far, though I am a bit intimidated by the math. Of course, it's just basic math for primary teachers, but, given my history of "math-itis" I can't help but anticipate struggles! Latin is a continuation of what I had at JCHS. The professor is antiquated and sometimes appears to fall asleep in mid conjugation. Being polite young ladies, we simply wait patiently for him to awaken. Some of the girls do avail themselves of the opportunity to take a peek at their compacts and powder their noses during his "naps".

I think college life is going to suit me! Thank you for the opportunity and for everything you have been for me. I will write more soon.

With love,

Ella Rose

Stokes, Gap, Tennessee 1919-1941

1933

Death of John

Family members and close friends crowded the Cummings home. "You can't stir 'em with a stick," Parthenia remarked.

John had gone out one day the previous week to hunt for the Oconee Bell. Ez went looking when dark was almost settled in and found the old man near the creek north of the ridge. John lay "peaceful-like with his hands folded on his chest" Ez reported. It was Ada's feeling, and Andrew's, that the doctor had died doing what he loved the most. Too bad that he never found that little flower.

Planning the funeral was complicated by the diaspora of grandchildren. Sad as the occasion was, it did afford Julian and Ella Rose and the young teenagers, Annette and Adaline, the opportunity to be together. The younger girls observed the other two as to what might be appropriate behavior when there was a death in the family. They were more apprehensive than grief stricken. They were appalled when someone mentioned Farley's name and both Ada and Parthenia began to cry. Definitely not appropriate, judging by the look on Mae's face.

1937

TELEGRAM

Andrew had received sporadic letters from Farley through the years and had responded but was never certain whether his letters were received. When their father died, he made every effort to locate his brother, knowing that effort was most likely wasted.

In 1937, he received a telegram stating simply:

Sick. Broke. Sorry. Can you wire a few dollars to W.U. office Knoxville? F.

When Andrew told Mae about the wire, she expressed her feelings, "of all things, pumping you for money when he has turned his back on your poor mother all these years."

"I know, but this is the first time in over 25 years he has actually reached out to any of us. He's my brother, Mae. What would you have me do?"

"If you send him more than $5, he will be after you for more and, if you resist, you won't hear from him again for another 25 years. I know how this type of person operates."

"I was not aware you had experience in dealing with down and out relatives, my dear," Andrew replied.

"Well, not MY relatives certainly, but one hears from friends all the time about such free-loaders."

Andrew wired back:

Stay put. Will respond soonest. A

Two days later, Andrew drove to Knoxville before dawn. He bought breakfast at the Regas Restaurant and started walking down mostly deserted Gay Street to the Western Union office. He noticed a man with a familiar gait walking toward him about a block away. When he looked again, the man had crossed the street and was heading west down a cross street. Following an instinct, Andrew jaywalked across Gay right in front of an approaching street car and sprinted down Cumberland Avenue in pursuit of the man who walked like his father. The man was moving very quickly. "Farley, Farley, stop. I know it's you." Instantly, the man stopped and sat down hard on the sidewalk, head in his hands.

Out of breath, John slowed his pace. "How in hell did you find me," Farley mumbled.

"I was going to camp out at the Western Union office as long as I needed to, to try and waylay you. But never mind that. Come on. Let's get you something to eat."

The brothers were greeted by curious glances when they made John's second visit to the Regas in one morning. Two middle-aged men of similar size, one with dark hair turning grey and the other with red hair turning white. John was respectably, if not handsomely, dressed. Farley's clothes were formerly rather flashy but now dirty and worn. As they walked past the counter, at which some few lingered over a late breakfast, heads were turned and noses were wrinkled at the smell emanating from

Farley, unwashed body, alcohol, and other, unidentifiable foulness.

They collected Farley's small bag at the flophouse and started out for home with no debate. En route, Farley told John that he had received word of their father's death, weeks after it occurred. "I would not have come anyway. They couldn't have stood the sight of me, crying like a baby for the father I cursed."

"I believe he would have forgiven you. There's pretty much nothing any of my children could do that would make me turn them away. Same with a brother. You chose to go, remember." Then, fearing he may have added to Farley's dejection, he added, "Father could be a hard case. That's for sure."

Along the way, Farley dozed off and on. In between naps, he told John of having been refused for the army in 1916 because of weak lungs. The irony immediately struck John.

"I did pretty damn well for a number of years, selling iceboxes and other things all over for Herrick. I could drive the Dollarway from Memphis to Little Rock blindfolded! Even had a wife and a little girl in Paducah. Our Dorothy died in '28 and Marjory fell apart. Started going out with other men and all until I left her. I couldn't take it."

He told John that he was able to make a living for another year or two until the Depression became full blown. Since then, he had just rambled and scraped and hoboed.

Farley cried and begged John to stop somewhere for a bottle. Andrew stopped for the bottle.

"Your wife won't want me in her house," Farley said.

"No, she won't. She sure won't. What we have to do is get you well. I want you to have a complete examination. God forbid you have T.B. I am going to put you up in a boarding house in Bristol for a few days, and then I'm going to put you in Southwestern State Hospital in Virginia. Figuring out what to tell Mae, and Mother, and Parthenia is the thing I can't cipher out yet."

"Well, thank you for at least having figured out my life. Just let me out right here, Andrew. Thanks for the breakfast and the bottle."

"Oh, simmer down. Do you really want to stay as miserable as you've been all these years? You're going to have to see some more misery in order to get better. Can't you do that for Mother?"

"God, I hate to think of how she'd feel if she could see me."

"Precisely why we're going to get you cleaned up. For her sake, for yours, and for Parthenia and Ez."

"Old Ez and Thenie. Still around huh?"

"Oh yes, them and their daughter still on the place. More family to mother than I've been able to be, to tell you the truth."

"Daughter? You mean Parthenia was finally able to foal? Good god."

"Sure did, and she's a fine one."

"A looker huh?"

"Hah. Not exactly. Not at all, in fact. But she's the best thing ever hatched on that farm. Mother loves her at least as much as she loves my kids, probably more. Having Ella Rose around was the only thing that kept her from grieving herself to death after you left."

Here, Farley began to cry again.

Farley did not have tuberculosis, but he was seriously malnourished. He was "dried out" at the hospital, but it took several months for him to rehabilitate sufficiently for Andrew to feel comfortable in presenting him to the folks at home. During visits at the hospital, Andrew realized he felt as much sympathy for the family members of patients as he did for the patients themselves. The elderly spouses of now demented sweethearts, the mothers of men never recovered from shell shock during the war and, in particular, one young woman he saw sobbing as she leaned against a wall after visiting her mother. He asked if he could do anything for her. She looked up at him without answering.

"I'm a doctor. I just thought you might need to go somewhere and sit down and have a glass of water."

"You are a doctor here? Will you open a window so my mother can jump out and kill herself?"

"Oh, dear. How long has she been here?"

"Off and on for years. Oh, don't mind me. It's just hell for me coming here."

"Will you be all right? I am not on staff here. I am visiting my brother. Things are getting better for him."

"Thank goodness at least one person gets better. I am all right. I'll be heading home now. Thank you for your concern. Truly."

This encounter stayed with Andrew. He hoped he would never need to go back to that hospital once Farley was released. He thought it the saddest place in all the world.

Soon, Andrew made a visit to Stokes Gap to prepare his mother and the Allisons for the news. He had not slept well for a week, anticipating how to best present what was bound to be a shock to them.

"Why didn't you bring Mae and the girls?" was Ada's first question.

"I just reckoned I wanted to spend some time with you all on my own for a change," Andrew responded, sitting down at the kitchen table. Parthenia and Ella Rose were there, and they anticipated Ez coming in at any moment.

"You going to stay all night?" Parthenia asked. "What should we make him for supper, Miz Cummings?"

"I could prepare that new recipe I clipped out of the Women's Home Companion," offered Ella Rose.

"He don't want none of that stuff. When a country boy comes home, he wants what he had as a young'un. Ain't that right Andrew?"

The women noticed Andrew didn't seem to be paying any attention to their lighthearted conversation.

"Honey, you're about as nervous as a long-tailed cat in a room full of rocking chairs. Whatever is the matter?" Ada asked.

"Well, where is…." Andrew started to say with a raised voice.

Just then Ez walked in.

"Howdy, howdy Dr. Andrew! How are you? Tickled me to death to hear you was coming to visit. Is this some kind of important meeting?" Ez said lightly.

Clearing his throat, Andrew began, "As a matter of fact, yes, it is, Ez. A few months ago, I heard from Farley."

Ada and Parthenia gasped. Ella Rose looked quizzical. Ez's face had gone instantly from jovial looking to utterly serious.

"Before you all start asking questions, just let me get out what I need to say. Ella Rose, you have heard us speak of Farley through the years. He is, of course, my brother, who left home under most unhappy circumstances before you were born."

"Oh, where is he? Where is he?" Ada begged.

Andrew said, "Mama" using a childhood name she had not heard for years, "he is over in Rossville right now. He has been very ill but has made a lot of progress. He feels terrible shame about his past. I have tried to tell him that everyone can forgive him, but he has not forgiven himself and is in a pretty fragile state of mind."

Ella Rose glanced nervously from her mother to her father. She knew better than to question Ada's response, but she had heard both bitter and nostalgic words about Farley.

"I want you to consider whether any of you might want to visit him in Rossville or at my house," Andrew continued.

"Lord God! Bring him home!" Ez exclaimed.

Autumn 1941
Stokes Gap

The St. Louis Cardinals had won the World Series in 1934, the year after John died. Ez could not stop talking about how John would have loved it. The Cardinals had a long dry spell, and Ez had had multiple strokes in the ensuing years. Any mention of the Yankees was likely to bring on another one, and the Brooklyn Dodgers were nearly as despised. In 1941, the Yankees had won the World Series again, a matter of much distress for Ez. Sadly, now unable to express his frustrations in words, he, nevertheless, made harsh and vociferous noises from his bed in the dining room, where the radio sat safely outside his reach.

The family could hardly remember what life had been like before they got the radio. Poor as reception was, even Ada was not deterred from fiddling with the knobs in an attempt to bring in WOPI more clearly, especially when Jack Benny was on. Now that baseball was finished, the radio provided entertainment more to the women's liking. Ella Rose was a big fan of the singer Dennis Day. She thought him "a dreamboat." She never missed the Jack Benny show when her idol was part of the program.

Ella Rose was by now a veteran of eight years teaching Home Economics at her alma mater, Johnson County High School. Perhaps as a result of her obvious handicaps, but more importantly because of her personality, her students considered her a safe confidante. Many days, a girl or two would linger after class or appear at the end of the school day to have a chat with Miss Allison. Most of their concerns were quite minor but Ella Rose treated them with the utmost seriousness and confidentiality. Over the years there had been two or three instances of pregnancy or assault. These very real crises were handled gently, with relatively positive outcomes for the most part. As a result, Ella Rose's standing in the community was unparalleled. Among the older adults, her gifts as a teacher and advisor were always attributed to the influence of Ada Cummings, rather than to her humble parents.

Although she enjoyed her work, at 30 Ella Rose was feeling a bit restless. She often thought of undertaking a new challenge, perhaps even moving out of Stokes Gap to a small city where she might make more sophisticated friends and enjoy cultural opportunities. In the midst of her fantasies, however, she would always stop and harshly remind herself of the obligations she had to her invalid father, her aging mother, widowed Ada, and unsteady Farley. She had come to believe that they all depended on her and that merely indulging in what-ifs was pure selfishness. The result was a slight but pervasive depression which she tried her best to conceal.

One Sunday evening in late autumn, after completing her lesson plans for the following week, she settled with Ada and Parthenia in the dining room to enjoy Benny and Day. Ez was dozing in his bed, but roused himself when he heard the crackling of the radio as Ella Rose sought the station.

They barely noticed the kitchen door opening and only tucked their feet in to make way for Farley, who now lived on his own in the cabin, take his place in their circle. Ez grimaced a sort of smile and grunted, "Er ee is."

"The Jell-O Show" began. Parthenia picked up the shirt she was turning the collar on from her mending basket. Dennis Day began to sing. Then the broadcast was interrupted to summon all lawmen and servicemen to their respective headquarters.

"What in heaven's name?" Ada asked as they studied each other's faces.

"Another damn War of the Worlds you can bet. Not a bit funny anymore," Farley declared.

That thought was minimally reassuring as the program resumed. Shortly, the announcer broke in again to bring the "war news." The Cummingses and Allisons only then learned about the bombing of Pearl Harbor. Sensing their alarm, Ez became fretful and began thrashing about in his bed. Parthenia tried to calm him but to no avail. Ada, especially, was always most distressed when Ez had one of these spells of agitation.

"Here. Y'all go on in the kitchen. I'll handle him," said Farley to the women. He sat down next to Ez and, patting him on the knee, he pulled his harmonica from his pocket and began playing <u>The Great Speckled</u> <u>Bird.</u> Ez was quickly soothed, but the larger world would not soon be.

PART IV

Knowledge of the self is the mother of all knowledge. So it is incumbent on me to know my self, to know it completely, to know its minutiae, its characteristics, its subtleties, and its very atoms.

Khalil Gibran

1950
<u>Recollections of Mattie Renfro</u>
Clayton Hill, Virginia

I reckon I know as much about the Grahams as anybody, except maybe other Grahams, which, Lord knows, there is a heap of. I've been living in Clayton Hill since I was a young girl and working for Hayden and Ginna Graham off and on for years.

Me and my husband Stub was from over in Darby Kentucky. Stub come here to work at the Barrel Works in 1910. Then, the next year, he come up home at Christmas time and carried me down here and married me. I was just 15 so they all figured I was in trouble but the truth was I couldn't wait to get out of Darby and out from under my mama and daddy. Why no, I wasn't in trouble.

Stub worked for Mr. Hay's daddy. We moved into the house I still live in to this day, down in the holler behind the Barrel Works. Maybe because I was so young I tried extra hard to keep my house and yard up. My mommy never had nothing, except nine babies, and it took me and her both just to look after them. So when I got my own house, I was very particular about everything. Knew how to cook and clean and grow a garden and can and did all that and waited for my own babies to start coming. Something is wrong with me. Some women just can't get that way because something is wrong inside.

But I didn't figure that out for quite a while and I just kept up my little company house, and Stub brought home his pay and we was happy. March 9, 1913 I was washing the kitchen floor when I heard steps on the porch. A lot of steps. The door flew open and I saw two men carrying Stub like he was sitting in a chair made of their arms. He was laughing like he felt foolish, and he did look right foolish. But a rag was wrapped around the shank of his left leg and some blood was soaking through.

"Stave come loose off the machine and stuck right into my leg, Matt," he said, like it was the most comical thing he ever heard.

"He is just trying to get to lay around the house and let you take care of him. Ain't nothing wrong with him. Give him a dose of

Castor Oil and see if that don't get him up and moving. Never did see a man so bad to play sick." That was from Jesse Burnop, Stub's friend. He loved to try to make Stub mad, but nobody could do that.

I said, "Let me get you cleaned up and see how bad it is," I said, rolling up his britches leg.

Jesse or Frank Painter, one, said "Mr. Graham says for him to stay home and keep his leg propped up today." Why, we all thought it was some kind of a holiday. His leg wasn't bleeding much, and he kept saying it didn't hurt a bit.

Jesse and Frank joked a while longer and went on back down to work. Stub kept his leg propped up like Mr. Graham said and played at being a invalid, and I went back to my floor washing and checked on him and petted him every little bit. We laughed about what a joke it was on Mr. Graham to be so worried about him. At dinner time, I made us a pan of cornbread and we ate a good meal of it and some canned tomatoes. Stub dozed on the bed while I cleaned up the dishes and did some ironing. Pretty soon, Stub woke up and talked me into the bed with him for a spell.

Jesse and Frank and Claude Forester came by after work to check on Stub, and they kept up the joke of him playing sick. We were all having a play party.

A week later, I buried Stub back in Darby. Blood poisoning set up in his leg, and even Dr. Thorpe couldn't seem to help him. My man suffered something awful for three days and nights before he died. The last night, after Dr. Thorpe had checked in on him and give him some laudanum to try to ease him, Stub started up to crying. "Matt" he said, "I am not saved. I never did get saved. I'll go to hell." I tell you, the blood in my veins turned to ice, and I thought to my soul I was going to be sick right there on the bed where Stub laid. I tried hard as I could to get myself in hand, but the tears started pouring out of my eyes. Stub couldn't see; he was too far gone to see anything or hardly even hear. Finally, I managed to say, "Stub, honey, you ain't going to hell. But, if by some chance you do, I swear to you, I'll come to hell and find you and either bring you out or stay there with you. I swear it to you now." And I will, too. Don't want to go to no heaven that would bar Stub, the best man ever lived, saved or not. Anyway, he went off to sleep and died before the sun had quite come up.

When I came back to Clayton Hill after the burying, intending to pack up my few little bits and pieces and drag them up to Mama's, I didn't hardly know I was in this world. I couldn't seem to think what I would do in Darby but I had no place else to go. Jesse's wife and Zula Painter and some of them would come by to sit with me a while and help me wrap up a few things. I wasn't hardly even polite to them, guess I never offered them a cup of coffee. I just sat there trying to puzzle out how to get stuff ready to go but my mind wouldn't stick on nothing. I reckon it was really them packed my few little boxes. My oldest brother Ruben was coming down to get me the next day and carry me back home. I was sitting on one of them boxes I remember, thinking I'd about as soon go ahead and start hunting for Stub than stay on this earth without him, when I heard a knock on the door. Figured it was Zula bringing a bite to eat so

I said "Come on." Didn't bother to get up and go to the door. I was a pitiful human if there ever was one.

The footsteps coming through the front room weren't made by no woman's feet. Nor no man's work boots either. I looked up to see Mr. Hayden Graham, the boss's son, standing in my kitchen. Except it wasn't my kitchen. It was more like HIS kitchen since it was a company house. I remember two things about that visit; I remember it felt like I had something gritty like sand in my teeth-had been feeling that way for two days. And I remember he said "Mrs. Renfro." I'd never been called Mrs. Renfro and I couldn't hardly tend to what else he was saying because I kept hearing "Mrs. Renfro" in my head.

Mr. Hay was a young fellow, maybe around 30, but he always did seem younger than me. He was a fine-looking man in a way but in a kindly soft way. He didn't have the, well I reckon the *bearing* of a man. Just a little bit backward. Don't mean he was no sissy-type man, just soft is the only word I can think of. He ain't changed.

Anyway, Mr. Hay said he come to tell me that him and his pap, the old Mr. Graham, wanted me to know that I could stay on in the company house just as long as I cared to. He said that what with how good a worker Stub was for them and how he come to die, they felt like they owed it to his widow to provide her with a roof over her head as long as she needed one. Now I didn't go to crying and carrying on. Like I said I was just a pitiful nothing sitting there on that box. Mr. Hay said that, if and when I had a mind to, there would be a plenty of jobs around Clayton Hill and that folks would be more than willing to hire me.

All in the world I was able to do was say "thank you kindly" and see him to the door. I came back and pulled the quilt out from one of the boxes, wrapped it around me and laid down on the floor and slept so hard I forgot all about poor Ruben coming to get me.

Soon after, Mr. Hay came down to ask if I felt up to coming up to his house and helping with his wife and baby. I had already heard about Mrs. Virginia Graham and her having a odd turn. I wasn't sure I wanted to be dealing with such but how could I refuse when the Grahams had been so good to me on account of Stub?

When I went up to the house a day or two later, I was surprised to find Mr. Hay still home. He said, "Now, Mrs. Renfro, Ginna, uh, my wife, has days when she doesn't feel well and days when she is quite well. It's a bit unpredictable, you see. Of course, what with a baby and all, she gets awfully tired. Some nights he keeps her up, and we no longer have the nurse who helped right after Baby Hayden was born."

It was just then I laid eyes on her for the first time. She came down the steps dressed to go to town. From head to toe, she was like some lady in a magazine.

"Hello, Maddie. I am Ginna. 'So glad you are going to be helping me with the baby. He is down for his morning nap and should sleep for an hour or more. Bottle is in the icebox. I'll be home after lunch."

With that she was gone and her husband said, "as you see, today she is very well indeed."

So that's when I started working for the Grahams. I worked for other folks too down through the years, but the Grahams was my main family. You better know that most all the ladies would try to get me to talk about Miss Ginna. That went on for years, even after she went into the hospital. The ladies knew that I knew everything that went on in that house. I believe they were jealous of her and loved to see her take one of her spells and cut a shine that they could talk about among their selves.

One time, Mrs. Yardley Brummit says, "Tell me, Mattie, does she ever talk about that first baby, the one they sent away?" I let on like I didn't know a thing about it, and, tell the truth, I am not rightly certain of the facts of it, but that question's been whispered around for as long as I have known the name Ginna Graham.

I was there to help when Frances was born in '16. Miss Ginna had a real bad time for nearly six months and couldn't hardly tend to the baby or Little Hay, who was two. She got some better and back into her outings and such. When the Spanish flu come through, nothing would do her but to run out taking care of people and putting together food boxes for them that was quarantined. Mr. Hayden and me was scared silly that she would bring that fluenza home to the children. He could not stop her, and she worked herself to a perfect nub by the time the second wave of it had done passed.

Little hellion Bascom was born around Christmas time in 1918. It's a wonder how she got that way and managed to carry him. I have pondered the Lord's will ever since. Never was a meaner child. I reckon the war straightened him out some, but he is still bad to drink and get into fights. I worry that one of these days he'll lose a fight and we'll end up burying him. He don't come around his poor old daddy much.

The baby Henry came along in 1925. I couldn't love him more if he was my own. Poor little fellow. What mothering he had, he got from me and maybe some from his sister Frances.

When she was having one of her spells of misery-they could last for months-Miss Ginna would beat on her own face, saying she killed her pap, and cry and carry on about her lost baby and wonder what become of him. Now, this was never in front of the children. I don't guess they ever knew about it. It seemed an awful shame to me that, while she was grieving over that one, if there was such a one, those she had right under her nose went around like orphans, just hungry for any kind of mothering at all. I didn't know back then that her pap died right after she got married and supposedly had the little boy that was give away. Well, I never did try to prowl about in her business, just soothe her the best I could.

Mr. Hay never seemed to budge from that way of his, like a cow in the pasture chewing its cud. Never mad. Never sad as far as I could tell. Just content to let me take care of the young'uns and fix his supper and keep his house. He treated Miss Ginna like she was the Queen of England or Mrs. Astorbilt. He was happy just to breathe the same air as her whether she was laying up in the bed all day or running around town stirring things up.

November 1931
Home from School

Frances drug her feet along the path between the Olingers'
house and her own front door. In spite of her bragging to Leola
that she was not "going to bother with the damned Latin"
homework, she knew for sure that she would be working on it an
hour from now. It was warm for November, and Frances felt
more draggy than usual on the way home from school that day.
She had an incipient blemish smack in the middle of her chin.
She knew it was going to be one of those bad ones that she
wouldn't be able to resist bothering and making even worse.

Head down as she scuffed along the front walk, she didn't look
up until she had almost reached the steps. "What are you doing
here?" she asked little brother Henry, who was sitting on the
next to top step, picking a scab on his knee.

"Door's locked. Mother must not be back from her meeting."

"You try the back door? It's never locked."

"Yep, I couldn't get it open neither."

"*Either*. Let me try. Quit that nasty picking. You are disgusting." Lately Frances had become quite fond of the word *disgusting* and Henry had picked it up from her. He grinned at her and rolled his pants leg down to cover up the now bleeding scab.

He followed her around the house to the back porch. They went through the screen door and, stepping over older brother Bascom's boots and Henry's skates, Frances used her years of experience and most of her 140 pounds to force open the stubborn back door.

Mother's pocketbook was on a kitchen chair. Frances maneuvered herself around in hopes Henry wouldn't notice it. Using her hip to slide the chair further under the table, she said, "How about a jelly biscuit, Master Graham?" Immediately she saw that that was the wrong thing to say.

"I'll wait for Mother."

There were no lights on in the stairway or hall and, because all the bedroom doors were closed, it was quite dark upstairs. Frances entered her parents' bedroom without knocking and saw exactly what she expected. Ginna was fully dressed, lying on her stomach, with the edge of the bedspread pulled up over her from the side. Her eyes were open.

"Mother, you feeling sick? Henry and I are home, and Daddy should be here after while. It's so warm outside. I've got a lot of homework. Mrs. Trent had a hissy fit because Ted Shelton made a rude sound. It was so funny. Leola's mother let her go to the picture show on a school night. Gold Diggers. Then

Leola tries to show me she can dance like Ruby Keeler or somebody. It's ridiculous," Frances chattered.

After a long silent moment, Frances asked, "Mother, do you want anything?" as she backed away from the bed.

"Close the door."

"Come on Henry. Let's us go visit Mattie. Get your coat on. It's getting cool." Henry grabbed his jacket from the doorknob and was out the door before Frances can pull her sweater on.

In less than five minutes, they made their way down the road to the block of company houses known locally as The Lane. Mattie didn't answer her front door so they headed around back.

"Get out of here, you sons of bitches," Mattie was hollering, as she heaved a bucket of water at two hound dogs. "Them scraps is for my cat. Stay off of my blessed back steps, you hear me?"

Turning to see Frances and Henry, Mattie smiled from ear to ear. "Why, look coming here. My babies." She swooped at Henry and mashed his head to her bosom.

"Matt, I think Daddy will be wanting you to come up to the house this evening. Mother's not feeling well." Saying this, Frances glanced down at the back of Henry's head.

Without missing a beat, Mattie released the boy and said, "Well, your daddy is going to be one happy man because I have got greens cooking and he will founder hisself. Let me just drain some of the liquor off and wrap a towel around the pot and we'll head up the hill. Now, Henry could you come here and get a little bite more for the cat to eat before we go? Them neighbor dogs stole her supper, and she's so nervous she doesn't know where to light. She's partial to you, and she'll eat if you sit and pet her some. Then we'll go on up and get y'all some supper on the table. How 'bout that?"

December 1931
<u>Julian Cummings Visits the Grahams</u>

As Christmastime neared, Ginna seemed a little better on some days. Occasionally, she would join the family for dinner, prepared, of course, by Mattie, but she spent most of the day in bed with the door closed. Hayden left every morning for the Barrel Works, came home at lunch, and returned to work for the afternoon as had been his routine their entire marriage. Even Frances was by now familiar with the pattern of her mother's illness and anticipated that, sooner or later, she would come home from school one day to find Ginna enthusiastically involved in a new interest, no one alluding to the spell of gloom they had all passed through.

Bascom, at thirteen, only stayed within the confines of the house when absolutely required to. His school marks reflected his inattention to scholastics and his body the evidence of fierce competition in any activity involving physical contact with his pals. Even his knuckles and posterior showed the marks of the ruler and paddle wielded by teacher and principal.

Mattie knew that as soon as Ginna was again "at herself" there would be no need for her to help out as much. Meanwhile, Henry stayed underfoot every minute he was not at school. He did not have the experience, or at least the clear memory, of his mother's nervous fluctuations. He complained of stomach aches, picked his scabs, whined and acted "babyfied" in Mattie's words.

One evening at supper, Hayden read a letter from Hayden Jr at college.

December 9, 1932

Dear Folks,

Well, it won't be too long now until I will be back in the fold for a good long Holiday. I will surely be glad to be out from under all this studying for awhile. Maybe I can get gone by the time you learn of my marks and decide that I have not been studying near enough. HA HA.

How is everyone? Only Frannie has written to me lately.

If it's all right, Mother, I would like to have a friend come visit after Christmas. He is from Tennessee and is a junior. He's on the debating team that I hope to join next semester. Awful swell fellow and should make a civilized guest. His name is Julian Cummings.

Tell Bascom that Julian can teach him a thing or two about boxing.

I had better close for now and turn to my biology notes.

Yours, Hay

P.S. I reckon I will be needing some money to buy my train ticket, or I could hop a freight with the hobos. HA HA.

Ginna didn't react. Bascom said, "he won't teach me nothing about boxing. Maybe he will teach Frannie something about K I S S I N G, if he's blindfolded first."

"Shut up, stupid," Frances said, setting a dish of pickled beets on the table.

"Goodness, you two, if just anticipating a visit is causing this commotion, I don't think we can survive the actual event. You should apologize to your mother."

Ginna was rubbing her knife vigorously with her napkin.

"Here comes the chicken and dumplings," Mattie announced through the swinging door.

Two days later, Ginna was a whirlwind of Christmas planning, decorating, and baking. The house had never been so elaborately done up for the holiday season. She even talked of holding open house for friends and neighbors to meet Hay's college friend.

Henry was gleeful to have his mother in good spirits, but Frances was frightened by the abrupt turn around. Mattie was still needed because of the frenetic preparations. Neither Bascom or his father seemed to notice.

Christmas day came and went, and Ginna's anticipation of the house guest's arrival caused more stir. Hay met Julian at the train late on Tuesday night. Assuming everyone was asleep, the two crept carefully up the stairs to Hay's room. They were awakened several times during the night by footsteps in the hall. Hay whispered, "my brother Bascom, trying to spy on us. Sorry. Go back to sleep. I'll kill him in the morning."

When they went down to breakfast in the morning, Hayden Sr. introduced himself to Julian and had little else to say. Bascom,

Frances, and Henry stared rather rudely at the visitor. Julian did not notice the lack of manners by the father and the children for he was enveloped in a storm of attention from Ginna. Dressed and coiffured to a level unprecedented for such an early hour, she asked him so many questions that he barely was able to swallow a bite between polite answers. "What are you studying?"; "How do you like what you have seen of Clayton Hill?"; "Can I get you some more marmalade?" and, coyly, "Does our Little Hay conduct himself like a gentleman at college?"

Until now, Hay had always seemed oblivious to his mother's odd behavior whether she was virtually shut away from the family or flamboyantly active in their midst. This was different. Of all the people he would want to make a good impression on Julian was foremost.

"Hey, Julian, we better get a move on if we are going to ride out to see the falls," he said, standing up and pushing his chair in with half his breakfast uneaten on the plate.

Julian, having heard nothing of this plan and rather enjoying being the focus of his friend's mother's interest, was momentarily at a loss for words. "Oh, yes. Well, thank you very much for the breakfast, Mrs. Graham." Turning to the rest of the family, he said, "Mr. Graham, uh, I guess we will see y'all later."

For the next two days Hay kept Julian as occupied and away from the house as possible. They went to movies, skeet shooting, sledding, and even, in a moment of desperation, to the library. Ginna continued to pepper Julian with questions during the brief times they were together, but Hay had become uncharacteristically talkative in an effort to keep her quiet. The younger children observed wordlessly.

The idea of an open house had been scratched, much to everyone but Ginna's relief, but they were having a nice dinner for New Year's Day with only sister Olivine and one or two of Hay's high school friends invited. Mattie was doing most of the cooking but Ginna was preparing two special desserts, her bread pudding and a chess pie.

"Frances, honey, why don't you change your blouse and comb your hair? It won't hurt a thing to look nice for your Aunt Ollie and your brother's friends. Get some of my pressed powder and see if you can hide those awful bumps on your chin." Frances rolled her eyes and slumped against the drain board.

"Well, start setting the table. Mattie and I can't do everything." Everything seemed to be precisely what Ginna was attempting to do. The best dishes were to be used. She had stayed up half the night ironing her grandmother's tablecloth and napkins, rarely used because they were so fragile.

When Olivine arrived an hour later, she stared grimly at the finery. "Ginna, Lord help us, you'll wear yourself out. Why all the fuss about a farm boy from Tennessee?"

"Ollie, you know I like to do things right and, what's more, make things special for my children and their friends." Ollie's eyes caught Fran's momentarily.

"Where are all them boys?" Mattie asked.

"Hay and Julian took the car over to pick up Calvin. I don't think Sam is coming," Frances commented. "Daddy's taking a walk."

Shortly, the front door opened and the three young men, talking and laughing, were greeted by the women.

"Olivine, this is Little Hay's college friend, Julian Cummings, and, of course, you know Cal," Ginna said as they found seats in the front room. "Julian, this is Hay's Aunt Olivine. Mattie and Frances are putting dinner on the table, and we'll eat just as soon as my husband returns from his ramblings."

Finally, seated at the table, the group numbered nine: Hayden and Ginna, Olivine, Hayden Jr, Frances, Bascom, Henry, Julian and Calvin. Ginna glanced at Hayden, who said, "Let's return thanks."

Following the blessing, he raised his water glass and toasted, "Here's to 1933. May it be a hell of an improvement on 1932."

Ginna said, "Hayden!" and the young people tittered.

Hayden carved the ham and passed plates around.

"This china belonged to our grandmother, Mary Graham. It was hidden in the cellar for years to keep the Yankees from smashing it. I believe it was ten years after the end of the war before they could convince her the threat had passed!" Olivine directed this comment to Julian with a smile. All the others, except Calvin, had heard this story a hundred times.

"I am confused. Your grandmother was a Graham, Mrs. Graham, and Miss Graham?" Julian said in genuine consternation.

"That's right. It is hard to follow, but our father and Hayden's father were cousins. Isn't that right Hayden?"

Hayden said, "Hmmph."

Hayden Jr said, "The truth is the Grahams marry each other because nobody else is good enough."

His parents and Aunt Olivine glared at him simultaneously while Frances and Bascom stifled giggles.

"That's why we all look like this," Bascom remarked, crossing his eyes and letting his tongue hang out for a minute.

"Ahmm. Now, Julian tell us about your family. Presumably, they offer a little more variety of surnames?" Ginna said. "I have been meaning to ask you more about them."

"My father's family are all around Stokes Gap over in Tennessee. Granddad was a doctor like father, but Granddad was as much a farmer as a doctor. Mother and father met in Nashville. She is originally from Kentucky."

"You say your father is a doctor?" Ginna asked.

Ginna's face colored as she glanced quickly at Olivine. "Did he, by any chance, study here, under Dr. Thorpe right after medical school?"

Hayden's attention was summoned at last. Now he looked helplessly at Olivine and back at Ginna.

Julian said "I don't know ma'am. Father is not one to talk much about his past or anything else. I think he did work under an older doctor for a short time but don't know where that was."

Ginna was on the verge of asking another question when her husband decided to enter the conversation. "Calvin, how do you like Lincoln Memorial? And what are you studying?"

Ginna had stopped eating and kept looking at Julian.

Calvin said "I like it pretty well, Mr. Graham, but I am not going back after the end of this term. Dad needs me to help him, and the tuition and books are pretty dear he says. So I'll stay out for a while."

"I am sorry to hear that, Cal. It's happening to more and more of us. Frances has her heart set on going to Hollins but she may have to wait tables if there's any chance of Bascom going to college. Never mind Henry." Hayden, having made his contribution to the conversation, resumed eating but glanced at Olivine to take up the gauntlet.

"It would have been 1910, Julian. Let's telephone your father and find out," Ginna blurted.

"Well, there are plenty of successful men who never attended college, isn't that right Hayden?" Olivine interjected half way through Ginna's comment, but Ginna was not diverted.

"His first name was Andrew! Is that your father's name, Julian?"

Now Julian looked from Hayden to Hay to Olivine, sensing that the urgency Ginna was expressing was making them uneasy.

"Long distance is too expensive. Julian can let us know after he writes to his father. Frances, pass the pickled beets please. Would anyone like another roll?" Olivine pleaded. "Save room for Ginna's wonderful desserts. Our mother's bread pudding and good old chess pie." She smiled ridiculously at everyone around the table.

Ginna sat silent with her hands in her lap for the rest of the meal as talk dwindled to awkward exchanges between Olivine and the young people.

January 14, 1932

Dear Mrs. Graham,

I apologize for the delay in thanking you and your family for the visit at your home at the New Year! My only excuse is that I was waiting to hear back from Dad as to whether he had any connections to Clayton Hill. Yes, his given name is Andrew, but he is known around here as Andy. He did study under an older doctor, he says, around 1909 or so, but that was in Beckley, West Virginia, I believe. He asked me to tell you that he very much hoped your association with the other "Andrew Cummings" was a pleasant one! My stay in Clayton Hill was a great deal of fun, and I will never forget your hospitality, the wonderful food, and conversation. Please give my regards to Mr. Graham and Miss Graham and to the "little" Grahams.

Hay is hitting the books for examinations and trying to make me do likewise. He is a good influence.

I look forward to seeing the family again. Many thanks for a swell time.

Sincerely,
Julian Cummings

Not many months later, following the death of John, Andrew made a reluctant confession to Julian.

"I have been wanting to speak with you about something. It's been bothering me a great deal. After you visited your friend, you asked me some questions about my earliest days in medicine. Well, mm, I'm afraid I was not truthful with you."

Julian had never been so shocked. His father was nothing if not compulsively truthful, sometimes to the distress of family members and patients. Before Julian could respond, his father continued, "I *was* in Clayton Hill, Virginia back in 1910. I believe I knew your friend's mother. For reasons I would rather not discuss, it is best that she not be made aware of that connection." Now Julian's shock turned to horror. What was his father implying? At 21, Julian was worldly enough to know that there were things men had to keep secret about their youths if they were to maintain the respect of their wives and children. But, surely not his father. His heart pounded and his face reddened.

"Nothing for you to concern yourself about. Just, please do not ever let on that I did know the Grahams. That was a sad time for several of us, and it wouldn't behoove anyone to dwell on it."

As it happened, Julian was already moving on from his college friends, and, so, would not likely have to be in a situation where the subject arose. His conjuring up of what his father may have meant became a matter of rumination for quite some years as he navigated his way into manhood and measured his own code of conduct.

1934-1935

Frances Goes to College

Julian Cummings did not visit the Grahams again, and Hay did his best to deflect Ginna's inquiries about him, saying only that Julian had graduated and moved off "to a job somewhere." Still, Ginna attempted unsuccessfully to ferret out information about the Cummings family from anyone she thought might be an acquaintance in common.

Frances graduated from high school. All she could think about was going away to college. The attention her mother gave to her departure for Hollins was so unprecedented that Frances hardly knew how to react.

"We must get you a winter coat and a spring coat and at least one more basic skirt and, oh, some presentable underwear," Ginna said, as she surveyed the clothing Frances had laid out on her bed. "You can't just go about indifferently the way you have here in Clayton Hill. You are going to be meeting a lot of quality girls, and, yes, boys."

"Hollins is a girls' school, Mama," Frances joked, hoping to continue the conversation.

"I know that, silly, but you will have dances and parties with boys from VMI and UVA and other good colleges. You know I want to you excel in your classes and go on to be a wonderful teacher or writer or whatever you want to be, but the truth is that many girls meet their husbands during the college years. You won't have to settle for marrying the first boy from here who comes to hand or, God forbid, become an old maid."

Aunt Ollie, who was in the room for this discussion, bit her tongue to keep from asking Ginna why *she* had married "the first boy who comes to hand." She didn't want to set Ginna off but was so furious that she pretended a need to check on something downstairs.

"Listen, my dear daughter, while we are talking frankly, let me say this: You have got to make the most of your good qualities. Not every woman can be a great beauty, but you have wit and charm, when you choose to reveal them. For heaven's sake,

218

wash and set your hair every week, put on some powder and even lipstick, throw your shoulders back and smile. That will make all the difference in your chances. You will see."

While her mother was excited about her going to college, her father only expressed a little concern about having a second child, a girl at that, in college, when many of his peers could barely keep a roof over their heads. Fran wasn't sure whether her father had genuine financial concerns or was covering up other feelings. Both her young brother Henry and Mattie turned down the corners of their mouths when mention was made of Frances' leaving. Though Frances was worried about missing home, and especially Henry, she did her best to keep from thinking about it.

For the first several weeks at Hollins, Frances struggled with the burden of classroom assignments for a while, but fell into a pattern of going to the library in the late afternoons so that she had more time to be silly with her dorm mates in the evenings. One of her professors made her uncomfortable with his iconoclastic attitude toward Southwestern Virginia values. He even thought that Franklin D. Roosevelt was the salvation of the country. Her father would be aghast. This is what college was supposed to be about, she reasoned, and began to feel more worldly.

When she went home for her first weekend visit in October, however, she was brought abruptly back to the reality of Clayton Hill and the Graham family. Bascom had been suspended from school for necking with a girl in the gymnasium. Mattie was not feeling well. Henry was heartbreakingly glad to see her. Ginna barely emerged from her bedroom during Frances's stay. Her father seemed older and didn't present his usual degree of insouciance about the situation. Frances only hoped that her Christmas holiday would dispel her concerns.

1934
<u>Letter of Referral</u>

Clayton Hill Virginia
November 28, 1934

Dr. C.W. Ketchum
Southwestern State Hospital
Rossville Virginia

Dear Dr. Ketchum:

This letter will accompany a patient I refer to you for mental evaluation, Mrs. Virginia Graham.

Mrs. Graham has been my patient since her childhood, along with her family. She is 50 years old, in reasonably good physical health, except for slightly elevated blood pressure. The reason for referral is that Mrs. Graham, having occasionally in the past been afflicted by periods of excitability or nervous depression, has recently experienced an aggravation of these symptoms, particularly the depression.

The patient is an intelligent lady from a highly regarded family. Her husband is the owner of Graham Barrel Works, and her father was Capt. George Graham. I expect you have heard of him. The patient and her husband are distant cousins.

Mrs. Graham was a rather nervous young person and married under unusual and distressing circumstances. I will explain more about that when I see you. As a mature woman, though most of the time an active member of the community, she has suffered episodes of melancholy that have kept her from caring for her children and household.

This autumn, with her two oldest children in college, a younger son has gotten into trouble. After a recent incident which involved the school authorities, Mrs. Graham became deeply troubled and slipped into a state of nervous depression. She has given up all personal hygiene, having previously been proud of her appearance. As in other times of illness through the years, a faithful housekeeper has stood in for Mrs. Graham in taking care of the children. For the past week, the patient has refused to eat.

As you will learn from her, if and when she comes around, Mrs. Graham becomes fixated on her maternal history and also the death of her father, and these two preoccupations lead to thoughts of suicide. Her history has been that, after coming out of these painful spells, she is happy, energetic and ready to rejoin the living, as it were, though, I must say, more inclined to engage with friends than with her family members, who suffer during both situations.

I have come to the end of my scant knowledge of matters of the mind and no longer feel adequate to treat Mrs. Graham. Thank you in advance for anything you can do for her. I will anticipate hearing from you as regards her condition and proposed treatment at your earliest convenience.

With sincere regards,

C. E. Thorpe, MD

1935-36
Frances at the Barrel Works

Ginna stayed at the hospital through Christmas and into the early spring. All members of the family were able to visit her there after the first of the year. She insisted to each of them that there was no reason whatsoever for her to remain, that she was "rested up" and ready to get back to Clayton Hill.

By the time Frances came home after her freshman year, she had concluded that she would not be continuing her education at Hollins. When she brought the subject up with her father, expecting some protest, he immediately acquiesced, saying that he needed to be able to send Bascom off to school the following year and, without Frances' tuition going out, that would be much more likely. Ginna, on the other hand, now feeling in charge of her household, objected violently. For a few weeks, she assumed she had brought Hayden and Frances around to her opinion.

They did not debate the matter with her, letting her think she had won the argument. They expected that, before the summer was over, her attention would have turned to some other matter.

In August, Mattie made a dramatic announcement: "Doctor Thorpe says I am going to have to have my womb took out." She had been resisting his advice for months but had grown so weak that she often needed to cut her workday short.

"Well, you just take care of yourself, Mattie. I can manage without you as long as you need to recover. When is your operation?" Ginna asked, while Frances and her father tried to envision weeks or months without Mattie to keep the household running. Even if Ginna remained "healthy," catastrophe would loom over them in Mattie's absence.

The surgery was scheduled for two weeks hence. Finally, Frances tentatively mentioned to her mother that she should perhaps skip at least the first term of her sophomore year. To her surprise, Ginna responded, "We will have such fun together, cooking and gossiping. We will show your daddy how well we

225

can manage without Mattie! I want us to do some sewing, and I will teach you to play bridge!"

Soon after Mattie left, Ginna's enthusiasm waned but she didn't mention Frances' schooling. Mattie's recuperation was slower than expected, and, for some time, even Dr. Thorpe was concerned that she might not fully recover. It was Frances who took meals to Mattie. More often than not, these culinary efforts benefited the cat, but Mattie was touched by Frances's concern.

"I have ate so much liver, I never want to taste another bite of it," Mattie declared when she was finally able to return to work. "Purely nasty."

With Mattie back on the job, Frances soon became bored. She had no interest in returning to college. That winter, her father made a proposal. "Frannie, how would you like to come help me out at the Works? Miss Cullop has gotten too old to work, and I really can't afford to hire a new girl. Of course, I would pay you some, but not what I have been paying Cullop all these years."

"Gosh, Dad, what would you want me to do? I can type a little, but I don't have any other office training."

"I don't think it would take long for you to pick up what I would need you to do. We'll take it slow."

So, in January 1936, Frances went to work for her father. Most of her high school friends were either already married, or working, with a handful having gone to college. Ginna was involved with her church ladies' activities. Both Ginna and Hayden held their breath that Bascom would stay out of trouble long enough to graduate from high school and head off to college, from which their oldest son was to graduate in the spring. Eleven-year-old Henry was a quiet child, though a close observer might have described him as *sad*. He had few friends, avoided Bascom stringently, and shadowed Frances during the evening hours.

Ginna was pleased when a young man, whom she considered "quality," began to call on Frances. His name was Ed Finley, and he was distantly related to Ginna's mother's family, the Comptons.

Frances had no experience with men, but she did have a pretty good idea of how she should feel around an attractive one, and she most certainly did not feel that way around Ed. She went out with him but invented all sorts of maneuvers to avoid that first kiss. Ed, not being very assertive, did not seek to force his unwanted affection on Frances, but the matter hung like a ghost between them when in each other's company.

Ginna tried to pry information out of Frances regarding this courtship. Even Hayden seemed to want it to flourish.

"He may not be your idea of Prince Charming, Frances, but he has a good job and is from a good family. He may not be handsome, but let's be realistic. You could do worse," Ginna offered by way of motherly advice.

Frances felt like a slightly defective heifer a farmer was trying to unload at the livestock market.

At work, though, she felt increasingly comfortable. She was soon able to perform all the tasks required of her and found to her surprise that she enjoyed working with both the customers and the employees. Most customer relations were handled by letter or telephone; her father was pleased with her facility at communication.

The six employees were all relatively young men, with one exception. They were only too glad to have a job during this Depression and never risked displeasing Hayden. At first, they were careful around the boss's daughter, but, as time passed, they began to relax and include her in their kidding each other. When her father was not around, Frances learned to give as good as she got, surprising the men with language she had learned from her older brother but would never use around her parents or aunts.

One day, Mattie said, "Frances, you need to watch out for them boys at the Works. They might try to toady up to you to get on Mr. Hay's good side."

For the first time in her memory, Frances was angry with Mattie. She was trying to rob Frances of the innocent pleasure she took in having friends at work. "What would you know about it, Matt? You never worked at a business. The fellows respect me. Maybe they even like me!"

1936

The Dew Drop

Frances had heard references to the Dew Drop since her high school days. It was a road house south of Clayton Hill considered disreputable by the reputable members of the community though Frances knew that some of her more daring contemporaries among the "better" families had ventured there and implied they had tales to tell. Prohibition had been repealed almost three years earlier, but, of course, Carver was a dry county. The livelihood of a number of folks in the area was dependent upon this fact remaining the status quo.

A man named Fleetwood Haynes was considered to be the most trustworthy purveyor of bootleg whisky. There were tragic stories about unfortunate happenings among those who chose to patronize less upstanding sources. Fleetwood might not be classified among the elite of Carver County, but his grandson went on to be elected delegate to the Virginia legislature some thirty years later and proudly represented his constituency in attempts to block desegregation in the public schools. His children and grandchildren *were* classified among the elite in the late 20th and early 21st century.

In 1936, most men, other than Baptists, had a standing account with Fleetwood. Little Hay had visited the establishment several times, but It was not that the Dew Drop sold whiskey. That was brought in the floorboards of cars in brown paper bags. The allure of the roadhouse was the opportunity to mingle freely with others who were enjoying Fleetwood's offerings, to dance and smoke and laugh and flirt.

Among Frances' work mates, there were frequent references to the "Drop," and, beginning to feel, as she did, one of the gang, Frances developed a deep interest in experiencing it. She knew her parents and Mattie would disapprove so she had to come up with a cover. She assumed she would be welcome to accompany her friends as soon as she could arrange to be available.

Finally, Ginna and Hayden planned a weekend trip to visit Aunt Louisa and her husband Leland in Damascus. Henry would accompany them, much against his wishes. Frances declined based on the pretext of needing to check in on the ailing Mattie. She tried to appear casual when she mentioned to Woodrow Thayer that she was thinking of going to the Drop on Friday night. She maintained the casual façade when Woodrow suggested that she catch a ride with him and another co-worker, L. W. Sims and some other friends. She thought of little else the rest of the week.

She would ask her friend Leola to advise about a dress. A veteran of the Dew Drop, Leola was now engaged and would be out to the picture show with her fiancé that night. That was just as well with Frances. Leola's presence at the Drop would have made her self-conscious. On the other hand, Leola was her main source of wisdom about the ways of the adult world in Clayton Hill. On Wednesday evening, Leola came to the house, and they went through the possibilities of a becoming outfit for Frances. "I swear, Frances, anyone would think you set out to remind the boys of your old maid aunts," Leola had often said in the past.

"I can't wear the heels. I'll be looking at the tops of their heads," Frances answered in response to Leola's telling her to try her one pair of dress shoes with the least spinsterish dress.

"That's all right. They'll be looking straight at your two best assets. Believe me, they love that." Leola countered.

"Oh, lord. Don't say that." Frances shuddered at the thought of dancing with a man fixated on her chest.

"Seriously, though, all I am saying is to be proud of your height and all. Make 'em think they would be lucky if you were to look down at the top of their sorry heads. Your mama never apologized for her height, and, from what I've heard, she had the men slobbering over her, back in her day."

This made Frances very uncomfortable. "Okay, I'll wear the heels but no more talk of who will be looking at what."

Leola promised to come again on Friday afternoon after the family had left for their little trip to help Frances with her hair and face.

The carload heading toward the Drop was so crowded that two men were standing on the running boards, hanging on for dear life. Frances was wedged in the back between Woodrow's girl, Maxie Phelps, and L.C.'s sister Mary Nell, and some young boy she didn't know. It was too noisy for a conversation, and Frances was relieved.

Outside the shabby looking building, cars were parked at crazy angles, and some were already occupied by men and couples having a quick drink before returning to the smoky interior. Inside was as noisy as the car ride had been and smoky, unlike the car with the windows rolled down. Frances waited for the group to seek out a table and sit down and stood awkwardly as they greeted friends with much hilarity. She began to think how much more comfortable she would have been at home or even, God forbid, at Aunt Louisa's. "Damnation," she told herself. "Smile, if it kills you." Finally, several of the group settled into chairs around a table at the edge of the room. With the exception of L.C. and Maxie and Mary Nell, Frances didn't know their table mates, who seemed to be mostly young men from Salt Creek that Woodrow knew from somewhere. These fellows were talking and laughing among themselves and, though friendly enough, did not particularly engage with the Clayton Hill bunch.

"What? Sorry I can't hear you," Frances answered Mary Nell who was sitting to her right.

"Oh, I just said that I reckon you're the first Graham ever to darken the door of this place."

Vaguely offended, Frances yelled over the racket, "Ha. My brother is here all the time." That wasn't exactly true, but she resented the implication, or what she thought was the implication, that the Grahams were too good to be seen at the Drop. She wanted more than anything to be regarded as just one of the group.

The Drop's new jukebox was a huge attraction, and Frances tried hard to be able to hear the music. She wished they were closer to its source. She could feel the beat at least and tapped the foot that was painfully trapped in the dress shoe.

After a while, L.C. got up with Maxie and came around to yell into Frances' ear, "We are going out to the car for a little refreshment. Care to join us?"

"Well, I guess so," Frances replied, looking at Mary Nell to see if she was included in the invitation. Mary Nell had begun talking to one of the Salt Creek boys and shook her head.

When they came back inside after the "refreshment" Frances noticed that the atmosphere seemed a little friendlier. Instead of just tapping her foot, she stood against the wall and admired the dancers. She was not musical but she sure enjoyed the rhythms of the Dorseys and Guy Lombardo and swayed slightly to the melodies.

"Wouldn't that be a lot more fun with a partner?" one of the Salt Creek boys inquired.

"Not much of a dancer, I'm afraid," Frances replied.

"Oh, come on. I've got thick leather shoes. You can't do too much damage."

He introduced himself as Gerald Young, and they danced a couple of dances. Woodrow broke in and danced with her too.

Wow, thought Frances. I could get used to this.

Another intermission for refreshment followed, and soon Frances found herself dancing most every dance and feeling quite carefree and light on her feet.

Salt Creek Gerald asked her dance with her again. "Hang on. If I can find a nickel, will you see if <u>Red Sails in the Sunset </u>is on the machine? I love it."

"Ma'am," he said making a slight bow, "I will insist on supplying the nickel. Don't budge off the very spot on which you stand. Right back."

Their selection was about third in line so they danced to the other numbers. Meanwhile a scuffle broke out on the other side of the room, but no one paid much attention. Frances was aware of feeling a little bit off balance, but it was not a problem as long as she was holding onto Gerald. He was not particularly handsome, but he was definitely tall enough for her to lay her head on his shoulder.

"Hey, Ger, let's go get us a little sip," one of his friends called.

"Nah, we're waiting to get our nickel's worth," Gerald responded with a smile, and they danced on.

By the time, <u>Red Sails in the Sunset</u> played, Frances had decided maybe Gerald was pretty nice looking after all, and it felt good to have his arms around her.

"Let's go out to the car for a minute and get a drink. I am parched," he said.

She followed him to the friend's car, and they got in the back seat. A bottle was passed to them from the friends in the front. Frances knew she had had too much but she also believed she hadn't had nearly as much as everyone else.

The couple in the front left to go back inside. Frances was leaning with her back against Gerald's chest and his arm around her shoulder. He kissed her neck, and she felt intense shivers up and down her body. He turned her around and began kissing her mouth. She thought she would stop him in just another minute or two, just another kiss or two, but not quite yet. Then she felt his hand on her knee and then under her dress above her stocking. A powerful force was making itself known, and it was no longer possible for to her make any kind of rational decision. As he continued to kiss her, the force built. Helpless as a newborn baby to resist it, Frances surrendered. She leaned away for a second and then vomited all over Gerald, the floor and seat of the car.

"Goddamn," he shouted and got out of the car, continuing to curse and pull his jacket and shirt off.

"Get out of the goddamned car," he yelled, pulling her by her arms so that she almost fell over her own feet. Frances was crying and then vomited some more.

From somewhere Woodrow and L.C. and Maxie appeared. Maxie took Frances by the hand and led her around to the side of the building.

"Sit right down here on this stump. I'll be back," she instructed. She returned with a wet cloth and tried to mop the mess off of Frances's front.

"Shit. Just do the best you can, and let's get out of here," Woodrow demanded.

Frances continued to cry all the way back to her house. The car door was opened and she stumbled out. No one offered to walk her to the door. She pushed her way in through the back door and threw her purse on the floor. She pulled off her clothes and tied them in a bundle and put them on the back porch.

The next afternoon, when Frances was finally able to think, she realized she needed to do two things. First, she burned the clothes in the burn pile behind the house. Second, she headed off to Mattie's to make true her excuse.

"I'm doing just fine, but you're looking mighty peaked," Mattie said when Frances arrived. Mattie was sitting in her little front room with her feet propped up on a stool. "Sit yourself down and tell me what's got hold of you."

"Nothing, Mat, just the curse, you know."

"Never knew the curse to show up in a person's face before. You look like something the cat spit up."

Frances began to cry a little bit.

Mattie said, "It's all right, honey. You tell me if you want to. If you don't want to, why don't you lay down on my bed for a spell, and I'll make us a cup of tea. How does that sound?"

Frances did lie down, and Mattie covered her with a quilt, though the room was too hot for it.

"I reckon you'll be just purt as can be by the time your folks get home. They'll never notice a thing.

PART V

"Everyone who tells a story tells it differently, just to remind us that everybody sees it differently. Some people say there are true things to be found, some people say all kinds of things can be proved. I don't believe them. The only thing for certain is how complicated it all is, like string full of knots. It's all there but hard to find the beginning and impossible to fathom the end. The best you can do is admire the cat's cradle, and maybe knot it up a bit more."

Jeanette Winterson

The Grahams
1937-1942

Though Frances continued working at the Barrel Works, she did not socialize further with her co-workers. They were polite but distant with her after the fiasco at the Drop. She helped out with her mother when Ginna was able to be at home and had occasional dates with old classmates but no major romance. She began to smoke and went out from time to time to more respectable night spots where she became much better at calibrating her alcohol intake.

After finishing high school, Bascom also went to work at the Barrel Works, foregoing college. He had a very active social life which Frances envied and Mattie worried over. Their father's attention was solely focused on the hope that Ginna would permanently recover sufficiently to be with them without interrupting hospitalizations.

In January of 1938, Ginna was treated for minor injuries including a broken wrist, following an automobile accident. She had insisted on learning to drive and Hayden had relented to the extent of giving her a couple of lessons in a flat lot behind the Works. After the holidays that year she had become more and more insistent on continuing the lessons. Apparently awakened by hot flashes during the night, she had left the house in her nightdress and undertaken to drive into town over the snow-covered roads. The automobile crashed into a ditch, and a passerby found her hobbling up the road two miles from home.

Subsequently, Ginna was readmitted to Summit. Clinical notes included the following:

Having been diagnosed with involutional melancholia upon her first admission, patient admitted most recently following a minor auto accident, exhibiting profound depression. She remained virtually mute for some time. Patient's husband provided a good deal more information about her history. Such information may have abetted her treatment during her prior admission.

Mrs. Graham was a Graham before their marriage, a second or third cousin to her husband. She was the youngest daughter of several, with two younger brothers. To his recollection, she had been a lively and creative if somewhat nervous child enjoying mostly excellent health. She attended Anderson Female Institute and pursued artistic interests as a young, unmarried woman.

Mr. Graham reported that his wife seemed to adjust happily to married life but suffered serious postpartum depression after each delivery. Although she seemed to recover each time within four to six months, she did have some difficulty in dealing with the children. Fortunately, they have employed for years a reliable housekeeper.

The husband said that, at times, his wife would suffer from periods of insomnia during which she would walk the floor and accuse herself of failing her children.

Otherwise, she seemed most content in church and community activities in which she was quite prominent. My impression is that her husband never wavered in his support.

JK Adams MD

Over ensuing years, hydrotherapy, Metrazol shock therapy, and insulin shock therapy were employed in treating Ginna. Ever hopeful, Hayden and his family welcomed reports of improvement with most of these efforts. Sadly, however, during brief visits home, or even before leaving the hospital, Ginna would relapse, often showing more worrisome behaviors than before administration of the new protocol.

In the late winter of 1942 electroshock was administered on three separate occasions. It was initially believed that the results were encouraging. The doctors spoke cautiously of the possibility of the patient being able to visit home if the diminution symptoms continued.

Frances Visits Her Mother

"I think you'll find her improved. If this continues, we might even be able to bring her home…. for a visit at least," Hayden had said to the family several weeks ago. Frances was skeptical, but couldn't quite ignore the tiny voice of hope whispering in her ear. Hayden Jr and Bascom had volunteered for the service almost immediately after war was declared. Aunt Ollie and her father had visited Ginna and were able to share the news with her without, they thought, unduly upsetting her.

Frances drove her father's car the 30 miles to Rossville. Always before, she had accompanied her father or Aunt Ollie, but this time she was on her own. Her mouth was dry and her hands were slippery on the steering wheel. It was a beautiful early spring day when the tiny emerging leaves made the natural world seem somehow fragile.

Summit State Hospital had been built two decades after the Civil War. The elegant main building was considered the most imposing structure from Richmond to the Tennessee state line. The formerly named Summit Lunatic Asylum was known to every man, woman, and child in that corner of Virginia. Once, when they were small, Frances and Bascom had made a joke about the "inmates" there, and had been severely reprimanded by their mother. "Don't show your stupidity! You would be surprised to know of your very own relatives who have spent time here." Frances had never forgotten that rebuke and wondered if Ginna had had a premonition about her own susceptibility.

Frances recognized the two matrons at the ward desk. Straightening her shoulders, she said "Good morning. Here to see Mrs. Graham."

The two women glanced at each other for an instant. Then the one who Frances presumed to be in charge said, "Umm. She's not feeling the best today. Maybe you'd want to come back another time?"

"Well, I'm her daughter. I think it will do her good to see me regardless."

After a moment's hesitation, the matron said, "then you will need to visit with her in her room rather than in the dayroom. She has not been apt to get along with the other patients lately." Glancing back at her colleague, she continued "Nannie, you go on in and check on Mrs. Graham first and then take Miss Graham back if she is, uh, ready."

Watching Nannie retreat down the hall, Frances said, "Is she much worse than she has been?"

"It's just she's got something taken hold of her mind and won't let it go. You know she gets like that sometimes. I reckon this time is a little worse than some others. You sure you don't want to wait til your daddy can come?"

Frances was offended at the suggestion that she was not capable of dealing with Ginna. And she was terrified that she was not capable of dealing with Ginna.

Ginna was seated on the edge of the window sill, hands on her knees, staring at her shoes. Her hair was fuzzy all around her head, and the wrapper she wore was unbelted. She did not look up when Nannie announced, "Virginia, your daughter's here to visit. You be nice now."

Fran sat on the foot of the bed rather than on the one chair available. "Hello Mother," avoiding the requisite "how are you?"

"Daddy and Ollie and Henry send love. I am on my own. Gonna do some shopping downtown before I head home. There's a sale at Belk's," she chattered on, anxiously waiting for some response to allow her to gauge her mother's mood.

"Henry is the only one of my boys not to be over there waiting to be killed. I don't care about Belk's or Ollie or Mattie. How can I think about anything but my poor boys?"

"Hay and Bascom will be fine. They are officers. You should be proud of them. Daddy and Henry fuss every day about Henry signing up. Daddy won't hear of it," Fran offered.

"No. It's already too late to change it. My punishment."

"Mama, let me tell you some of the news from home. Betty Fletcher and Fred Beatty got married while he was home from basic training. Her name is Betty Beatty. Isn't that a mouthful? We're getting new hymnals finally. The old ones are falling to pieces. Of course, Mrs. Brummit objects to the color of the new ones, dark blue. What does she ever do but object to something or other? Oh, and Mr. Crane has been awful sick, something with his lungs, but not pneumonia. I can't remember. He's not in the hospital but poor old Dr. Thorpe is over at their house all the time."

"I wish all my children had been daughters instead of four boys. But God would have found some other way of punishing me. He would have found some other way."

"You have three sons and one daughter, and God is not punishing you for anything. Your illness is punishing you. Try to think of your blessings."

"Oh, shut up. Who are you? I did have a girl but I have four boys. What do you know?"

"Mama, I am Frances."

"Of course, I know that. All my boys but little Henry are over there waiting for God to strike them because of what I did. I wish he would strike me instead. I wish he would strike me now, this minute. I was beautiful, simply beautiful, and the men couldn't stay away from me. All those lovely young men. They were boys then too, and they fell down at my feet and begged me to love them. "

Ginna got very quiet and still. Frances held her breath and prayed the violently whispered madness would stop.

"It's all right Mother. It's all right."

"Because I was beautiful and I could not deny them, I killed my papa and sent my sons to war to be killed. Bascom and Hay and the other one."

"The other one is Henry, and all of them are safe."

"No. Not Henry. We don't know." Then she lay down her bed and turned to the wall.

Frances waited for an agonizing 10 minutes and with great relief assured herself that Ginna was asleep.

Driving home, she remembered echoes over the years of her mother's hints that she had caused her father's death and some references to lost loves or had it been lost children? She had never wanted to know, and she didn't want to know now. The very idea of asking her overburdened father for confirmation seemed cruel beyond contemplation.

Within weeks, Frances began to explore the possibilities of working in the nation's capital as all the papers proclaimed the need for assistance in the war effort. She found herself so energized that she was able to smother the memory of her last encounter with her mother.

Ella Rose Measures Up

The late summer of 1942 found Ella Rose in Baltimore at Johns Hopkins. An urgent call had gone out from Washington for suitable candidates to become dieticians for the anticipated returning injured veterans and subsequent hospital needs. Home economics teachers, especially single ones, were especially courted.

Ella Rose had submitted an application in April including only her pertinent education and work history. When school was out in early June, she was summoned to Baltimore for an interview and assignment to housing, with the presumption that she would be accepted. It never occurred to her that she would be eliminated because of her physical limitations, but from the facial expression of the receptionist when she arrived to the outrageously solicitous manner of the interviewer she quickly deduced that she would be needing her best Allison instincts to overcome the perception that she was not up to the job .

"Now, Miss Allison, it is readily apparent that you have excellent work experiences from your history of teaching home economics to young girls back down in Tennessee. I am sure you are very much at home in that role, amongst your family and friends. Let us explore a bit the prospects of navigating a hospital, interacting with veterans or other patients, difficulties of traveling, and so on."

"All right. Most certainly, let's explore. As to traveling, I note there are streetcars in Baltimore. I traveled here from Bristol Virginia by train on my own," Ella Rose said with a smile on her face that did not betray her pounding heart.

"I would imagine that you have been somewhat limited in dealing with the general public, outside your pupils" Dr. Black pushed on.

"It's true that Johnson County is hardly teeming with all stripes of humanity but I flatter myself that I have done pretty well handling the roughest hoodlums among the hallways of Johnson County High, not to mention close relatives of mine who are inclined to get pretty rowdy after consuming liquor. I have gutted deer and executed many a chicken. Have you ever chased a chicken around the backyard, Dr. Black? Not easy with this cane but it does have the advantage of the crook on the end which has come in handy for me a number of times."

"Men from backgrounds all over the country will be among our patients. Many, if not most, will lack the sort of manners that you are accustomed to. You would hear words that were never uttered in your presence. That sort of thing makes medical careers difficult for young ladies."

"I dare say I have heard from both my parents, shall we say, "earthy" expressions that would enlarge your potential vocabulary. Shall I try a few?" Ella Rose responded with a little laugh and the most charming smile she could radiate.

Two weeks later, she received notification of her acceptance to undertake an expedited course at Johns Hopkins to prepare her for a dietitian internship.

Encounter on the Train

The heat from the sidewalk outside Union Station radiated through the soles of Frances' spectator pumps. She knew without looking that her legs were streaked with orange as the leg make-up melted.

When she had finally managed to drag her suitcase through the sea of passengers and squeeze herself down the aisle to find a seat near the back of the train car, she wished to God she was anywhere else. All around her, people were juggling their boxes and grips, all grimly determined to stake a claim to their portion of this crowded vessel. Soldiers, who were given priority, seemed to be everywhere. A couple of them gave her the eye but she ignored them. How could they be so damned cheerful when, sooner or later, they would be heading to Europe or the Pacific?

After what seemed like hours, all the passengers were settled, or as settled as was possible given the heat and the noise and the shortage of space. "Train travel is always a thrill, isn't it?" Frances looked across the aisle to see the source of this absurd question. A queer, bird-like woman sat perched on her seat like a child on a swing, her feet several inches from the floor, a cane in her left hand scotching her position.

Try as she might, Frances could not manage to be downright rude, so she aimed for *distracted.* Looking out the window on her side of the aisle, she replied crisply, "At times."

"Where are you headed?" came the cheerful reply. Well, hell, Frances thought and, reluctantly directing her gaze at her fellow traveler, she tried once more, and more earnestly this time, to put to rest the prospect of further conversation by saying with an exaggerated sigh, "Just a quick trip home to deal with some family matters." Then, quickly settling herself as if to doze, she folded her arms across her middle, turned her head away and closed her eyes.

"Oh, I am going home too! I haven't seen my folks for two months, and I am so excited. Of course, I won't be staying long because I will be going to Illinois for further training and who knows how long I will be away next time. I will miss them terribly but they understand that, at a time of war, I am proud to do whatever I can to serve my country."

Frances opened her eyes and stared at the woman. Besides being tiny and obviously lame, she wore eyeglasses with the thickest lenses Frances had ever seen. It was hard to guess her age but Frances thought maybe a few years older than herself. Something about her face made its two halves seem mismatched, reminding Frances of a wax figurine which has been placed too near the stove causing one side of it to soften and slide downhill. There was nothing about this individual that suggested the remotest capacity to serve her country, or even take care of herself for that matter. Except for her beautiful auburn hair which was gathered up into curls on the top of her head a la Betty Grable, she seemed an object of pity.

Had she had the energy, Frances might have speculated to herself about the origin of this woman's illusion of fitness. All she wanted, however, was to get home to her father and brother in Clayton Hill, do what had to be done, and get the hell back to her job as a stenographer and file clerk with the War Department, to the tiny third floor apartment she shared with her roommate Carolyn, to her lover Bill and their bridge games and the excitement of Washington.

"I am sorry! My name is Ella Rose Allison...."

"Ummm. Fran Graham. Pleased to meet you."

"Where is your home Miss Graham? I am from Stokes Gap TN near Johnson City."

Frances felt a headache beginning in the middle of her forehead. And did she feel a twinge in her lower back? She made a mental inventory of the contents of her suitcase: a fresh blouse, her one surviving pair of stockings, nightgown, underwear, lipstick, comb, toothpowder and toothbrush, a tin of bobby pins, and yes, thank God, three sanitary pads just in case she had gotten off schedule.

"I'll be getting off at Marion. Uh, Miss Allison, it has been fun chatting with you but I am feeling awful tired, and we have a long day ahead of us. If you don't mind, I believe I'll try to take a little snooze."

"Certainly. You go right ahead and I will try to keep myself just quiet as a mouse over here. Sweet dreams!"

The Good Witch Glinda sat on a bench in a flower garden where daylilies, peonies, tulips and daffodils bloomed simultaneously. Chubby bluebirds flocked around her whistling the melody to Big Rock Candy Mountain. Beautiful Glinda stood and held out her hands and welcomed one of the whistlers to light there.

Glinda's bright gown turned dark. Suddenly, she was no longer Glinda but the beautiful and wicked queen, Snow White's stepmother. A cloud enveloped the scene. The queen began to rise above the ground. Her gown became the purple-black of a grackle's wings. As she rose higher, she became a bird but not a grackle. A bird with a mustard colored beak. She flapped her enormous wings to gain altitude but was very ungainly. High above the ground, in a lacy delicate tree like a willow, a nest, actually a worn straw garden hat turned upside down, held a famished family of baby birds. On hearing the approach of the big, clumsy bird, they raised their little beaks and squawked out pleas for a bite of food. The bird tried to land on the nest, seemed to gain purchase but after a few seconds the doomed hat-nest wobbled back and forth on its slender branch. Inevitably, the huge bird flew away, upending the nest and sending baby birds tumbling to the ground where they were pounced upon by waiting cats. The nest itself did not completely dislodge from the branch but was still attached to one or two tiny twigs, hanging parallel to the tree trunk, swaying more and more violently in the wind. A lone baby, its claw entangled in the hat's weave, hung helplessly upside down, its fragile leg its only tether to home...

Funeral

"Good Lord, are you driving?" Fran asked Henry at the train station, glancing around dramatically as if hoping to spot an alternative chauffeur.

"Well, who else? Daddy won't drive at night and Aunt Ollie sure don't. Who'd you expect... Mattie?" Henry grinned as he grabbed her suitcase. "Come on. I'll get you home safe."

To Fran, it seemed impossible that Henry had just turned 18, in spite of his being the family giant at 6'4". He would always be her baby brother. Henry had another year of high school and, thanks be to God, had not convinced their father to let him enlist. Having two older brothers in the service was surely enough for this family to have to offer up. There had been no question of either Hay or Bascom being able to get leave to come home.

Walking to the car, Fran lit a cigarette, took a deep draw, and stretched both arms up toward the starry sky. "It feels so good to be cool for a change. Washington is hot as hell, and the train was worse. I swear I have never been so miserable as the last 8 hours. Felt like the other people were just sucking the breath right out of me. Crazy woman in the seat next to me. Good Lord."

As they drove the 3 1/2 miles to their home in their father's Plymouth sedan, purchased shortly before the war, Fran asked Henry about school and his friends but got little information. Their joy in being together, despite the ostensible sadness of the occasion, was hard to suppress as they vied in teasing each other in the old familiar way.

But, climbing the steps to the back-porch Fran felt for a moment the awful feeling she had on the train when she woke up from that horrible dream. Then, the screen door opened and Mattie stood square in the light of the kitchen.

"I can't hear myself think for them jar flies. Come on in. Your daddy and aunt barely got their eyes open. How was the train?" Being greeted by Mattie's shower of words immediately soothed Fran's nerves. "Henry, I got your suit pants let out and pressed. They're ahanging on your door knob. I'm heading for the house. Be here first thing."

"Matt.......'night," Fran said, reluctant to let her go but aware of how many hours she must have spent manning the kitchen and its stream of visitors. Every square inch of the kitchen table was covered with the offerings of Clayton Hill cooks, and, no doubt, the icebox was bulging, rationing be damned.

"Hey, how about something to eat, Frannie? You name it, we got it," said Henry, playing the unaccustomed role of host to his sister.

"Not right now. Might fix me a ham biscuit in a while. Oh, Lord, what's this?" Fran said picking up the folded newspaper. Reading the front page of the weekly Daniel County News, she was quiet for a minute, then snorted, then grew quiet again.

Prominent Clayton Hill Woman Dies

Mrs. Hayden (Virginia) Graham died suddenly on Wednesday evening, from a stroke of paralysis, while visiting friends in Rossville. Funeral services will be conducted from the home on Saturday with Rev. H. W. Kilpatrick officiating. She will be laid to rest in the Clayton Hill Presbyterian Church Cemetery.

Mrs. Graham, a daughter of the late Col. George Bascom Graham, CSA, and the late Lettie (nee Compton) Graham, is well known for her contributions to the cultural and religious life of the community. She was a leading light of the Women of the Church of Clayton Hill Presbyterian. Mrs. Graham had been in declining health for some years.

Besides her husband, Hayden Graham, the deceased is survived by sons, Lt. Hayden Compton Graham and Lt. Bascom Graham,

**both serving in Europe, Henry Graham of the
home, and a daughter, Miss Frances Graham
of Washington City. Other survivors include
sisters Misses Flora and Pearl Graham of
Rural Retreat, Mrs. Jefferson Carter of
Maple Grove, Miss Olivine Graham of
Clayton Hill and brothers, Stuart Graham of
Clayton Hill and Charles Graham of Bristol.**

"Spose Daddy would notice if I took a swallow of his Early
Times?" Fran said to Henry, then straightened her shoulders
and made a noisily theatrical gulp as she went through the
dining room into the front room to greet her father and her aunt.

Shortly before 10:30 the following morning, the mourners began
to arrive. Every chair in the house, plus a few borrowed from
neighbors, filled the front parlor, where Virginia Graham
Graham lay in her casket. Most of the attendees had been to call
at the house the day before and, so, unlike Frances, had had the
opportunity to view the deceased. Aunt Ollie had tried to get
Frances to approach her mother soon after her arrival but Fran
had delayed, saying she wanted to be alone to say goodbye.
Both her father and aunt assumed that had taken place after they
went to bed.

Henry greeted folks at the door and showed them into the parlor while Frances was still taking the pin curls out of her hair in the bedroom. Should she wear lipstick?

"Ready Frances? They are filling up the front room," Aunt Ollie whispered through the closed door.

"Okey dokey, let's go," Fran said, taking Ollie's arm in hers as if the older woman needed assistance down the stairs. Frances kept her attention on Ollie to avoid looking at the curious, oh-so-sympathetic faces of her mother's contemporaries.

When they got to the parlor, rather than greeting mourners, Ollie said, "I need to see her one more time" and, thanks to her poorly thought out arm-linking tactic, Fran found herself staring down at an unrecognizable corpse with tightly curled hair, heavy powder and rouge, wearing a dove grey dress, her primly folded hands covered by a fine lace handkerchief. Insanely, Frances had the thought that her mother had not died after all. This body bore not the faintest resemblance to the being who was Mother.

In their last years Ada Cummings and Parthenia Allison were to spend many evenings recalling their memories of their years together in Stokes Gap. Because the most important memory could not ever be mentioned to anyone else, and because it was the one, they agreed, upon which the course of both of their lives had shifted, they especially relished recounting it over and over.

Reminiscences

It was in the winter of 1911. Farley had not been heard from for three years. Andrew's wedding to Mae was planned for April. In the dark, gloomy days they washed and ironed the best linens, polished the silver and dusted the baseboards, and Ada fretted about the house being presentable to Mae's folks, whom they were to meet in a few weeks. Ada worried about whether John would be gracious, or at least civil, to the future in-laws, whether Ez would stay away from the bottle, whether she could avoid becoming overwhelmed by all of it. The change of life was adding to her distress, and she was impatient with everyone, including Parthenia.

The two were sitting at the sheet-covered dining room table, polishing yet another batch of silver.

"I declare, I'd rather be beaten with a broom than fool with this silver, "Ada complained.

Parthenia did not say anything.

"Well, you aren't talking. I guess you thoroughly enjoy it, don't you?"

"Wouldn't go that far, Miss Ada, but it sure beats doing what Ez and Doc is doing right now," Parthenia said, hoping to prevent another snippy remark from her employer. She wasn't feeling all that well herself and was worried that, for the first time ever, she might spit out some impertinent words she'd regret.

Ez was mending fence, and John had gone to visit the Methodist preacher on a house call. Reverend Bancroft had requested that the doctor come to him as he was unable to sit in his buggy to come to the office.

"I suppose you are right. I would rather polish silver than lance a carbuncle on the preacher's backside," Ada conceded.

"That's for sure. Wouldn't care to be anywhere near the ass end of that feller," Parthenia returned. The tension was broken.

"Lands, I suppose I had better undertake that pitcher. Don't know why I don't do it first and get it over with. So many little swirls and curls" Ada said, more than half-hoping that Parthenia would grab it first.

In an instant they both looked up simultaneously when they heard the front door open and close. Before the women had time to become frightened rather than puzzled, they heard footsteps, parcels being placed on the floor and then "Mother?"

Andrew walked into the dining room as they continued to sit with their mouths open.

"What in the nation?" Ada said in a not very welcoming tone, for now she was truly alarmed about this unexpected arrival and *was afraid that Andrew had been dismissed by the doctor or Mae had broken their engagement.*

"Mother, I need to talk to Thenie. Would you please go into the kitchen?" Andrew said.

Ada's mouth went dry, and her heart raced.

"Mother, I am sorry but I don't have much time. I will explain later." He quickly kissed her cheek and waited while she got up from the chair and left him with Parthenia, who looked after her with stunned bewilderment.

"Thenie, over in Virginia where I am working, there has been a uh situation, a very sad situation. A child was born to an unmarried woman. The baby is very sickly. I don't know whether it can live. I don't think it can live. But I want it to have a chance." Parthenia recognized a look about Andrew's face that she had seen many times in his boyhood; it betrayed the supreme effort he was making to hold back tears.

"I got the idea that maybe you could...."

A mouse squeaked in the front hall. That's what Parthenia thought she heard for a second. The next second she stood up from her chair, 3 teaspoons clattering to the floor, and pushed past Andrew as he tried to rise.

In the hall, Parthenia fell on her knees beside the basket Andrew had left there. She unwrapped the layers of towels and blankets as painstakingly as if they were bandages on tender wounds and took her daughter in her arms for the first time...

Epilogue

Both Hay and Bascom survived the War. Hay married and had one child. Bascom was married and divorced twice. Frances married in 1949 and had three children in rapid succession. Mattie died in 1952 and was buried, not in Kentucky but in the Graham family plot in the church cemetery. Henry was buried next to her when he died by his own hand a year later.

Ella Rose became director of the dietary department of a large and well-known hospital in Minnesota. She had many close and rewarding friendships. She died in 1988 and is buried beside her parents in Stokes Gap.

Farley was able to go back to work in the Stokes Gap Bank during the War and stayed there until retirement. He married a widow and died in 1965.

Ada and Parthenia lived on together at the Cummings place until shortly after the War when Parthenia died and Ada moved in with Julian.

CPSIA information can be obtained
at www.ICGtesting.com
Printed in the USA
LVHW092139081019
633638LV00001B/71/P